The Blue Lagoon

The Blue Lagoon

Henry De Vere Stacpoole

MINT EDITIONS

The Blue Lagoon was first published in 1908.

This edition published by Mint Editions 2021.

ISBN 9781513283777 | E-ISBN 9781513288796

Published by Mint Editions®

 MINT
EDITIONS

minteditionbooks.com

Publishing Director: Jennifer Newens
Design & Production: Rachel Lopez Metzger
Project Manager: Micaela Clark
Typesetting: Westchester Publishing Services

Contents

BOOK I

PART I

    I. WHERE THE SLUSH LAMP BURNS   13

    II. UNDER THE STARS   16

    III. THE SHADOW AND THE FIRE   21

    IV. AND LIKE A DREAM DISSOLVED   24

    V. VOICES HEARD IN THE MIST   28

    VI. DAWN ON A WIDE, WIDE SEA   32

    VII. STORY OF THE PIG AND THE BILLY-GOAT   38

    VIII. "S-H-E-N-A-N-D-O-A-H"   41

    IX. SHADOWS IN THE MOONLIGHT   47

    X. THE TRAGEDY OF THE BOATS   52

PART II

    XI. THE ISLAND   57

    XII. THE LAKE OF AZURE   60

    XIII. DEATH VEILED WITH LICHEN   66

    XIV. ECHOES OF FAIRY-LAND   70

    XV. FAIR PICTURES IN THE BLUE   74

Part III

XVI. The Poetry of Learning 79

XVII. The Devil's Cask 87

XVIII. The Rat Hunt 91

XIX. Starlight on the Foam 94

XX. The Dreamer on the Reef 98

XXI. The Garland of Flowers 102

XXII. Alone 105

XXIII. They Move Away 107

Book II

Part I

I. Under the Artu Tree 113

II. Half Child—Half Savage 115

III. The Demon of the Reef 120

IV. What Beauty Concealed 123

V. The Sound of a Drum 127

VI. Sails Upon the Sea 130

VII. The Schooner 135

VIII. Love Steps In 138

IX. The Sleep of Paradise 141

PART II

X. An Island Honeymoon   145

XI. The Vanishing of Emmeline   147

XII. The Vanishing of Emmeline (continued)   151

XIII. The Newcomer   153

XIV. Hannah   155

XV. The Lagoon of Fire   158

XVI. The Cyclone   160

XVII. The Stricken Woods   163

XVIII. A Fallen Idol   166

XIX. The Expedition   168

XX. The Keeper of the Lagoon   173

XXI. The Hand of the Sea   175

XXII. Together   176

Book III

I. Mad Lestrange   179

II. The Secret of the Azure   181

III. Captain Fountain   183

IV. Due South   190

BOOK I

PART I

I

Where the Slush Lamp Burns

M r. Button was seated on a sea-chest with a fiddle under his left ear. He was playing the "Shan van vaught," and accompanying the tune, punctuating it, with blows of his left heel on the fo'cs'le deck.

> "*O the* Frinch *are in the bay,*
> *Says the* Shan van vaught."

He was dressed in dungaree trousers, a striped shirt, and a jacket baize—green in parts from the influence of sun and salt. A typical old shell-back, round-shouldered, hooked of finger; a figure with strong hints of a crab about it.

His face was like a moon, seen red through tropical mists; and as he played it wore an expression of strained attention as though the fiddle were telling him tales much more marvellous than the old bald statement about Bantry Bay.

"Left-handed Pat," was his fo'cs'le name; not because he was left-handed, but simply because everything he did he did wrong—or nearly so. Reefing or furling, or handling a slush tub—if a mistake was to be made, he made it.

He was a Celt, and all the salt seas that had flowed between him and Connaught these forty years and more had not washed the Celtic element from his blood, nor the belief in fairies from his soul. The Celtic nature is a fast dye, and Mr. Button's nature was such that though he had been shanghaied by Larry Marr in 'Frisco, though he had got drunk in most ports of the world, though he had sailed with Yankee captains and been man-handled by Yankee mates, he still carried his fairies about with him—they, and a very large stock of original innocence.

Nearly over the musician's head swung a hammock from which hung a leg; other hammocks hanging in the semi-gloom called up suggestions of lemurs and arboreal bats. The swinging kerosene lamp cast its light forward, past the heel of the bowsprit to the knightheads, lighting here a naked foot hanging over the side of a bunk, here a face from which protruded a pipe, here a breast covered with dark mossy hair, here an arm tattooed.

It was in the days before double topsail yards had reduced ships' crews, and the fo'cs'le of the *Northumberland* had a full company: a crowd of packet rats such as often is to be found on a Cape Horner "Dutchmen" Americans—men who were farm labourers and tending pigs in Ohio three months back, old seasoned sailors like Paddy Button—a mixture of the best and the worst of the earth, such as you find nowhere else in so small a space as in a ship's fo'cs'le.

The *Northumberland* had experienced a terrible rounding of the Horn. Bound from New Orleans to 'Frisco she had spent thirty days battling with head-winds and storms—down there, where the seas are so vast that three waves may cover with their amplitude more than a mile of sea space; thirty days she had passed off Cape Stiff, and just now, at the moment of this story, she was locked in a calm south of the line.

Mr. Button finished his tune with a sweep of the bow, and drew his right coat sleeve across his forehead. Then he took out a sooty pipe, filled it with tobacco, and lit it.

"Pawthrick," drawled a voice from the hammock above, from which depended the leg, "what was that yarn you wiz beginnin' to spin ter night 'bout a lip me dawn?"

"A which me dawn?" asked Mr. Button, cocking his eye up at the bottom of the hammock while he held the match to his pipe.

"It vas about a green thing," came a sleepy Dutch voice from a bunk.

"Oh, a Leprachaun you mane. Sure, me mother's sister had one down in Connaught."

"Vat vas it like?" asked the dreamy Dutch voice—a voice seemingly possessed by the calm that had made the sea like a mirror for the last three days, reducing the whole ship's company meanwhile to the level of wasters.

"Like? Sure, it was like a Leprachaun; and what else would it be like?"

"What like vas that?" persisted the voice.

"It was like a little man no bigger than a big forked raddish, an' as green as a cabbidge. Me a'nt had one in her house down in Connaught in the ould days. O musha! musha! the ould days, the ould days! Now, you may b'lave me or b'lave me not, but you could have put him in your pocket, and the grass-green head of him wouldn't more than'v stuck out. She kept him in a cupboard, and out of the cupboard he'd pop if it was a crack open, an' into the milk pans he'd be, or under the beds, or

HENRY DE VERE STACPOOLE

pullin' the stool from under you, or at someother divarsion. He'd chase the pig—the crathur!—till it'd be all ribs like an ould umbrilla with the fright, an' as thin as a greyhound with the runnin' by the marnin; he'd addle the eggs so the cocks an' hens wouldn't know what they wis afther wid the chickens comin' out wid two heads on them, an' twinty-seven legs fore and aft. And you'd start to chase him, an' then it'd be mainsail haul, and away he'd go, you behint him, till you'd landed tail over snout in a ditch, an' he'd be back in the cupboard."

"He was a Troll," murmured the Dutch voice.

"I'm tellin' you he was a Leprachaun, and there's no knowin' the divilments he'd be up to. He'd pull the cabbidge, maybe, out of the pot boilin' on the fire forenint your eyes, and baste you in the face with it; and thin, maybe, you'd hold out your fist to him, and he'd put a goulden soverin in it."

"Wisht he was here!" murmured a voice from a bunk near the knightheads.

"Pawthrick," drawled the voice from the hammock above, "what'd you do first if you found y'self with twenty pound in your pocket?"

"What's the use of askin' me?" replied Mr. Button. "What's the use of twenty pound to a sayman at say, where the grog's all wather an' the beef's all horse? Gimme it ashore, an' you'd see what I'd do wid it!"

"I guess the nearest grog-shop keeper wouldn't see you comin' for dust," said a voice from Ohio.

"He would not," said Mr. Button; "nor you afther me. Be damned to the grog and thim that sells it!"

"It's all darned easy to talk," said Ohio. "You curse the grog at sea when you can't get it; set you ashore, and you're bung full."

"I likes me dhrunk," said Mr. Button, "I'm free to admit; an' I'm the divil when it's in me, and it'll be the end of me yet, or me ould mother was a liar. 'Pat,' she says, first time I come home from say rowlin', 'storms you may escape, an' wimmen you may escape, but the potheen 'ill have you.' Forty year ago—forty year ago!"

"Well," said Ohio, "it hasn't had you yet."

"No," replied Mr. Button, "but it will."

II

Under the Stars

It was a wonderful night up on deck, filled with all the majesty and beauty of starlight and a tropic calm.

The Pacific slept; a vast, vague swell flowing from far away down south under the night, lifted the *Northumberland* on its undulations to the rattling sound of the reef points and the occasional creak of the rudder; whilst overhead, near the fiery arch of the Milky Way, hung the Southern Cross like a broken kite.

Stars in the sky, stars in the sea, stars by the million and the million; so many lamps ablaze that the firmament filled the mind with the idea of a vast and populous city—yet from all that living and flashing splendour not a sound.

Down in the cabin—or saloon, as it was called by courtesy—were seated the three passengers of the ship; one reading at the table, two playing on the floor.

The man at the table, Arthur Lestrange, was seated with his large, deep-sunken eyes fixed on a book. He was most evidently in consumption—very near, indeed, to reaping the result of that last and most desperate remedy, a long sea voyage.

Emmeline Lestrange, his little niece—eight years of age, a mysterious mite, small for her age, with thoughts of her own, wide-pupilled eyes that seemed the doors for visions, and a face that seemed just to have peeped into this world for a moment ere it was as suddenly withdrawn—sat in a corner nursing something in her arms, and rocking herself to the tune of her own thoughts.

Dick, Lestrange's little son, eight and a bit, was somewhere under the table. They were Bostonians, bound for San Francisco, or rather for the sun and splendour of Los Angeles, where Lestrange had bought a small estate, hoping there to enjoy the life whose lease would be renewed by the long sea voyage.

As he sat reading, the cabin door opened, and appeared an angular female form. This was Mrs. Stannard, the stewardess, and Mrs. Stannard meant bedtime.

HENRY DE VERE STACPOOLE

"Dicky," said Mr. Lestrange, closing his book, and raising the table-cloth a few inches, "bedtime."

"Oh, not yet, daddy!" came a sleep-freighted voice from under the table; "I ain't ready. I dunno want to go to bed, I—Hi yow!"

Mrs. Stannard, who knew her work, had stooped under the table, seized him by the foot, and hauled him out kicking and fighting and blubbering all at the same time.

As for Emmeline, she having glanced up and recognised the inevitable, rose to her feet, and, holding the hideous rag-doll she had been nursing, head down and dangling in one hand, she stood waiting till Dicky, after a few last perfunctory bellows, suddenly dried his eyes and held up a tear-wet face for his father to kiss. Then she presented her brow solemnly to her uncle, received a kiss and vanished, led by the hand into a cabin on the port side of the saloon.

Mr. Lestrange returned to his book, but he had not read for long when the cabin door was opened, and Emmeline, in her nightdress, reappeared, holding a brown paper parcel in her hand, a parcel of about the same size as the book you are reading.

"My box," said she; and as she spoke, holding it up as if to prove its safety, the little plain face altered to the face of an angel.

She had smiled.

When Emmeline Lestrange smiled it was absolutely as if the light of Paradise had suddenly flashed upon her face: the happiest form of childish beauty suddenly appeared before your eyes, dazzled them—and was gone.

Then she vanished with her box, and Mr. Lestrange resumed his book.

This box of Emmeline's, I may say in parenthesis, had given more trouble aboard ship than all of the rest of the passengers' luggage put together.

It had been presented to her on her departure from Boston by a lady friend, and what it contained was a dark secret to all on board, save its owner and her uncle; she was a woman, or, at all events, the beginning of a woman, yet she kept this secret to herself—a fact which you will please note.

The trouble of the thing was that it was frequently being lost. Suspecting herself, maybe, as an unpractical dreamer in a world filled with robbers, she would cart it about with her for safety, sit down behind a coil of rope and fall into a fit of abstraction: be recalled to life by the evolutions of the crew reefing or furling or what not, rise to superintend the operations—and then suddenly find she had lost her box.

Then she would absolutely haunt the ship. Wide-eyed and distressed of face she would wander hither and thither, peeping into the galley, peeping down the forescuttle, never uttering a word or wail, searching like an uneasy ghost, but dumb.

She seemed ashamed to tell of her loss, ashamed to let anyone know of it; but everyone knew of it directly they saw her, to use Mr. Button's expression, "on the wandher," and everyone hunted for it.

Strangely enough it was Paddy Button who usually found it. He who was always doing the wrong thing in the eyes of men, generally did the right thing in the eyes of children. Children, in fact, when they could get at Mr. Button, went for him *con amore*. He was as attractive to them as a Punch and Judy show or a German band—almost.

Mr. Lestrange after a while closed the book he was reading, looked around him and sighed.

The cabin of the *Northumberland* was a cheerful enough place, pierced by the polished shaft of the mizzen mast, carpeted with an Axminster carpet, and garnished with mirrors let into the white pine panelling. Lestrange was staring at the reflection of his own face in one of these mirrors fixed just opposite to where he sat.

His emaciation was terrible, and it was just perhaps at this moment that he first recognised the fact that he must not only die, but die soon.

He turned from the mirror and sat for a while with his chin resting upon his hand, and his eyes fixed on an ink spot upon the table-cloth; then he arose, and crossing the cabin climbed laboriously up the companion-way to the deck.

As he leaned against the bulwark rail to recover his breath, the splendour and beauty of the Southern night struck him to the heart with a cruel pang. He took his seat on a deck chair and gazed up at the Milky Way, that great triumphal arch built of suns that the dawn would sweep away like a dream.

In the Milky Way, near the Southern Cross, occurs a terrible circular abyss, the Coal Sack. So sharply defined is it, so suggestive of a void and bottomless cavern, that the contemplation of it afflicts the imaginative mind with vertigo. To the naked eye it is as black and as dismal as death, but the smallest telescope reveals it beautiful and populous with stars.

HENRY DE VERE STACPOOLE

Lestrange's eyes travelled from this mystery to the burning cross, and the nameless and numberless stars reaching to the sea-line, where they paled and vanished in the light of the rising moon. Then he became aware of a figure promenading the quarter-deck. It was the "Old Man."

A sea captain is always the "old man," be his age what it may. Captain Le Farges' age might have been forty-five. He was a sailor of the Jean Bart type, of French descent, but a naturalised American.

"I don't know where the wind's gone," said the captain as he drew near the man in the deck chair. "I guess it's blown a hole in the firmament, and escaped somewheres to the back of beyond."

"It's been a long voyage," said Lestrange; "and I'm thinking, Captain, it will be a very long voyage for me. My port's not 'Frisco; I feel it."

"Don't you be thinking that sort of thing," said the other, taking his seat in a chair close by. "There's no manner of use forecastin' the weather a month ahead. Now we're in warm latitoods, your glass will rise steady, and you'll be as right and spry as anyone of us, before we fetch the Golden Gates."

"I'm thinking about the children," said Lestrange, seeming not to hear the captain's words. "Should anything happen to me before we reach port, I should like you to do something for me. It's only this: dispose of my body without—without the children knowing. It has been in my mind to ask you this for some days. Captain, those children know nothing of death."

Le Farge moved uneasily in his chair.

"Little Emmeline's mother died when she was two. Her father—my brother—died before she was born. Dicky never knew a mother; she died giving him birth. My God, Captain, death has laid a heavy hand on my family; can you wonder that I have hid his very name from those two creatures that I love!"

"Ay, ay," said Le Farge, "it's sad! it's sad!"

"When I was quite a child," went on Lestrange, "a child no older than Dicky, my nurse used to terrify me with tales about dead people. I was told I'd go to hell when I died if I wasn't a good child. I cannot tell you how much that has poisoned my life, for the thoughts we think in childhood, Captain, are the fathers of the thoughts we think when we are grown up. And can a diseased father—have healthy children?"

"I guess not."

"So I just said, when these two tiny creatures came into my care, that I would do all in my power to protect them from the terrors of life—or rather, I should say, from the terror of death. I don't know whether I have done right, but I have done it for the best. They had a cat, and one day Dicky came in to me and said: 'Father, pussy's in the garden asleep, and I can't wake her.' So I just took him out for a walk; there was a circus in the town, and I took him to it. It so filled his mind that he quite forgot the cat. Next day he asked for her. I did not tell him she was buried in the garden, I just said she must have run away. In a week he had forgotten all about her—children soon forget."

"Ay, that's true," said the sea captain. "But 'pears to me they must learn sometime they've got to die."

"Should I pay the penalty before we reach land, and be cast into that great, vast sea, I would not wish the children's dreams to be haunted by the thought: just tell them I've gone on board another ship. You will take them back to Boston; I have here, in a letter, the name of a lady who will care for them. Dicky will be well off, as far as worldly goods are concerned, and so will Emmeline. Just tell them I've gone on board another ship—children soon forget."

"I'll do what you ask," said the seaman.

The moon was over the horizon now, and the *Northumberland* lay adrift in a river of silver. Every spar was distinct, every reef point on the great sails, and the decks lay like spaces of frost cut by shadows black as ebony.

As the two men sat without speaking, thinking their own thoughts, a little white figure emerged from the saloon hatch. It was Emmeline. She was a professed sleepwalker—a past mistress of the art.

Scarcely had she stepped into dreamland than she had lost her precious box, and now she was hunting for it on the decks of the *Northumberland*.

Mr. Lestrange put his finger to his lips, took off his shoes and silently followed her. She searched behind a coil of rope, she tried to open the galley door; hither and thither she wandered, wide-eyed and troubled of face, till at last, in the shadow of the hencoop, she found her visionary treasure. Then back she came, holding up her little nightdress with one hand, so as not to trip, and vanished down the saloon companion very hurriedly, as if anxious to get back to bed, her uncle close behind, with one hand outstretched so as to catch her in case she stumbled.

HENRY DE VERE STACPOOLE

III

The Shadow and the Fire

It was the fourth day of the long calm. An awning had been rigged up on the poop for the passengers, and under it sat Lestrange, trying to read, and the children trying to play. The heat and monotony had reduced even Dicky to just a surly mass, languid in movement as a grub. As for Emmeline, she seemed dazed. The rag-doll lay a yard away from her on the poop deck unnursed; even the wretched box and its whereabouts she seemed to have quite forgotten.

"Daddy!" suddenly cried Dick, who had clambered up, and was looking over the after-rail.

"What?"

"Fish!"

Lestrange rose to his feet, came aft and looked over the rail.

Down in the vague green of the water something moved, something pale and long—a ghastly form. It vanished; and yet another came, neared the surface, and displayed itself more fully. Lestrange saw its eyes, he saw the dark fin, and the whole hideous length of the creature; a shudder ran through him as he clasped Dicky.

"Ain't he fine?" said the child. "I guess, daddy, I'd pull him aboard if I had a hook. Why haven't I a hook, daddy?—why haven't I a hook, daddy?—Ow, you're *squeezin'* me!"

Something plucked at Lestrange's coat: it was Emmeline—she also wanted to look. He lifted her up in his arms; her little pale face peeped over the rail, but there was nothing to see: the forms of terror had vanished, leaving the green depths untroubled and unstained.

"What's they called, daddy?" persisted Dick, as his father took him down from the rail, and led him back to the chair.

"Sharks," said Lestrange, whose face was covered with perspiration.

He picked up the book he had been reading—it was a volume of Tennyson—and he sat with it on his knees staring at the white sunlit main-deck barred with the white shadows of the standing rigging.

The sea had disclosed to him a vision. Poetry, Philosophy, Beauty, Art, the love and joy of life—was it possible that these should exist in the same world as those?

He glanced at the book upon his knees, and contrasted the beautiful things in it which he remembered with the terrible things he had just seen, the things that were waiting for their food under the keel of the ship.

It was three bells—half-past three in the afternoon—and the ship's bell had just rung out. The stewardess appeared to take the children below; and as they vanished down the saloon companion-way Captain Le Farge came aft, on to the poop, and stood for a moment looking over the sea on the port side, where a bank of fog had suddenly appeared like the spectre of a country.

"The sun has dimmed a bit," said he; "I can a'most look at it. Glass steady enough—there's a fog coming up—ever seen a Pacific fog?"

"No, never."

"Well, you won't want to see another," replied the mariner, shading his eyes and fixing them upon the sea-line. The sea-line away to starboard had lost somewhat its distinctness, and over the day an almost imperceptible shade had crept.

The captain suddenly turned from his contemplation of the sea and sky, raised his head and sniffed.

"Something is burning somewhere—smell it? Seems to me like an old mat or summat. It's that swab of a steward, maybe; if he isn't breaking glass, he's upsetting lamps and burning holes in the carpet. Bless *my* soul, I'd sooner have a dozen Mary Anns an' their dustpans round the place than one tomfool steward like Jenkins." He went to the saloon hatch. "Below there!"

"Ay, ay, sir."

"What are you burning?"

"I an't burnin' northen, sir."

"Tell you, I smell it!"

"There's northen burnin' here, sir."

"Neither is there, it's all on deck. Something in the galley, maybe—rags, most likely, they've thrown on the fire."

"Captain!" said Lestrange.

"Ay, ay."

"Come here, please."

Le Farge climbed on to the poop.

"I don't know whether it's my weakness that's affecting my eyes, but there seems to me something strange about the main-mast."

The main-mast near where it entered the deck, and for some distance

HENRY DE VERE STACPOOLE

up, seemed in motion—a corkscrew movement most strange to watch from the shelter of the awning.

This apparent movement was caused by a spiral haze of smoke so vague that one could only tell of its existence from the mirage-like tremor of the mast round which it curled.

"My God!" cried Le Farge, as he sprang from the poop and rushed forward.

Lestrange followed him slowly, stopping every moment to clutch the bulwark rail and pant for breath. He heard the shrill bird-like notes of the bosun's pipe. He saw the hands emerging from the forecastle, like bees out of a hive; he watched them surrounding the main-hatch. He watched the tarpaulin and locking-bars removed. He saw the hatch opened, and a burst of smoke—black, villainous smoke—ascend to the sky, solid as a plume in the windless air.

Lestrange was a man of a highly nervous temperament, and it is just this sort of man who keeps his head in an emergency, whilst your level-headed, phlegmatic individual loses his balance. His first thought was of the children, his second of the boats.

In the battering off Cape Horn the *Northumberland* lost several of her boats. There were left the long-boat, a quarter-boat, and the dinghy. He heard Le Farge's voice ordering the hatch to be closed and the pumps manned, so as to flood the hold; and, knowing that he could do nothing on deck, he made as swiftly as he could for the saloon companion-way.

Mrs. Stannard was just coming out of the children's cabin.

"Are the children lying down, Mrs. Stannard?" asked Lestrange, almost breathless from the excitement and exertion of the last few minutes.

The woman glanced at him with frightened eyes. He looked like the very herald of disaster.

"For if they are, and you have undressed them, then you must put their clothes on again. The ship is on fire, Mrs. Stannard."

"Good God, sir!"

"Listen!" said Lestrange.

From a distance, thin, and dreary as the crying of sea-gulls on a desolate beach, came the clanking of the pumps.

IV

And Like a Dream Dissolved

Before the woman had time to speak a thunderous step was heard on the companion stairs, and Le Farge broke into the saloon. The man's face was injected with blood, his eyes were fixed and glassy like the eyes of a drunkard, and the veins stood on his temples like twisted cords.

"Get those children ready!" he shouted, as he rushed into his own cabin. "Get you all ready—boats are being swung out and victualled. H—l! where are those papers?"

They heard him furiously searching and collecting things in his cabin—the ship's papers, accounts, things the master mariner clings to as he clings to his life; and as he searched, and found, and packed, he kept bellowing orders for the children to be got on deck. Half mad he seemed, and half mad he was with the knowledge of the terrible thing that was stowed amidst the cargo.

Up on deck the crew, under the direction of the first mate, were working in an orderly manner, and with a will, utterly unconscious of there being anything beneath their feet but an ordinary cargo on fire. The covers had been stripped from the boats, kegs of water and bags of biscuit placed in them. The dinghy, smallest of the boats and most easily got away, was hanging at the port quarter-boat davits flush with the bulwarks; and Paddy Button was in the act of stowing a keg of water in her, when Le Farge broke on to the deck, followed by the stewardess carrying Emmeline, and Mr. Lestrange leading Dick. The dinghy was rather a larger boat than the ordinary ships' dinghy, and possessed a small mast and long sail. Two sailors stood ready to man the falls, and Paddy Button was just turning to trundle forward again when the captain seized him.

"Into the dinghy with you," he cried, "and row these children and the passenger out a mile from the ship—two miles—three miles—make an offing."

"Sure, Captain dear, I've left me fiddle in the—"

Le Farge dropped the bundle of things he was holding under his left arm, seized the old sailor and rushed him against the bulwarks, as if he meant to fling him into the sea *through* the bulwarks.

Next moment Mr. Button was in the boat. Emmeline was handed to him, pale of face and wide-eyed, and clasping something wrapped in a little shawl; then Dick, and then Mr. Lestrange was helped over.

"No room for more!" cried Le Farge. "Your place will be in the long-boat, Mrs. Stannard, if we have to leave the ship. Lower away, lower away!"

The boat sank towards the smooth blue sea, kissed it and was afloat.

Now Mr. Button, before joining the ship at Boston, had spent a good while lingering by the quay, having no money wherewith to enjoy himself in a tavern. He had seen something of the lading of the *Northumberland*, and heard more from a stevedore. No sooner had he cast off the falls and seized the oars, than his knowledge awoke in his mind, living and lurid. He gave a whoop that brought the two sailors leaning over the side.

"Bullies!"

"Ay, ay!"

"Run for your lives—I've just rimimbered—there's two bar'ls of blastin' powther in the hould!"

Then he bent to his oars, as no man ever bent before.

Lestrange, sitting in the stern-sheets clasping Emmeline and Dick, saw nothing for a moment after hearing these words. The children, who knew nothing of blasting powder or its effects, though half frightened by all the bustle and excitement, were still amused and pleased at finding themselves in the little boat so close to the blue pretty sea.

Dick put his finger over the side, so that it made a ripple in the water (the most delightful experience of childhood). Emmeline, with one hand clasped in her uncle's, watched Mr. Button with a grave sort of half pleasure.

He certainly was a sight worth watching. His soul was filled with tragedy and terror. His Celtic imagination heard the ship blowing up, saw himself and the little dinghy blown to pieces—nay, saw himself in hell, being toasted by "divils."

But tragedy and terror could find no room for expression on his fortunate or unfortunate face. He puffed and he blew, bulging his cheeks out at the sky as he tugged at the oars, making a hundred and one grimaces—all the outcome of agony of mind, but none expressing it. Behind lay the ship, a picture not without its lighter side. The long-boat and the quarter-boat, lowered with a rush and seaborne by the mercy of Providence, were floating by the side of the *Northumberland*.

From the ship men were casting themselves overboard like water-rats, swimming in the water like ducks, scrambling on board the boats anyhow.

From the half-opened main-hatch the black smoke, mixed now with sparks, rose steadily and swiftly and spitefully, as if driven through the half-closed teeth of a dragon.

A mile away beyond the *Northumberland* stood the fog bank. It looked solid, like a vast country that had suddenly and strangely built itself on the sea—a country where no birds sang and no trees grew. A country with white, precipitous cliffs, solid to look at as the cliffs of Dover.

"I'm spint!" suddenly gasped the oarsman, resting the oar handles under the crook of his knees, and bending down as if he was preparing to butt at the passengers in the stern-sheets. "Blow up or blow down, I'm spint—don't ax me, I'm spint!"

Mr. Lestrange, white as a ghost, but recovered somewhat from his first horror, gave the Spent One time to recover himself and turned to look at the ship. She seemed a great distance off, and the boats, well away from her, were making at a furious pace towards the dinghy. Dick was still playing with the water, but Emmeline's eyes were entirely occupied with Paddy Button. New things were always of vast interest to her contemplative mind, and these evolutions of her old friend were eminently new.

She had seen him swilling the decks, she had seen him dancing a jig, she had seen him going round the main deck on all fours with Dick on his back, but she had never seen him going on like this before.

She perceived now that he was exhausted, and in trouble about something, and, putting her hand in the pocket of her dress, she searched for something that she knew was there. She produced a Tangerine orange, and leaning forward she touched the Spent One's head with it.

Mr. Button raised his head, stared vacantly for a second, saw the proffered orange, and at the sight of it the thought of "the childer" and their innocence, himself and the blasting powder, cleared his dazzled wits, and he took to the sculls again.

"Daddy," said Dick, who had been looking astern, "there's clouds near the ship."

In an incredibly short space of time the solid cliffs of fog had broken. The faint wind that had banked it had pierced it, and was now making pictures and devices of it, most wonderful and weird to see. Horsemen

HENRY DE VERE STACPOOLE

of the mist rode on the water, and were dissolved; billows rolled on the sea, yet were not of the sea; blankets and spirals of vapour ascended to high heaven. And all with a terrible languor of movement. Vast and lazy and sinister, yet steadfast of purpose as Fate or Death, the fog advanced, taking the world for its own.

Against this grey and indescribably sombre background stood the smouldering ship with the breeze already shivering in her sails, and the smoke from her main-hatch blowing and beckoning as if to the retreating boats.

"Why's the ship smoking like that?" asked Dick. "And look at those boats coming—when are we going back, daddy?"

"Uncle," said Emmeline, putting her hand in his, as she gazed towards the ship and beyond it, "I'm 'fraid."

"What frightens you, Emmy?" he asked, drawing her to him.

"Shapes," replied Emmeline, nestling up to his side.

"Oh, Glory be to God!" gasped the old sailor, suddenly resting on his oars. "Will yiz look at the fog that's comin'—"

"I think we had better wait here for the boats," said Mr. Lestrange; "we are far enough now to be safe if—anything happens."

"Ay, ay," replied the oarsman, whose wits had returned. "Blow up or blow down, she won't hit us from here."

"Daddy," said Dick, "when are we going back? I want my tea."

"We aren't going back, my child," replied his father. "The ship's on fire; we are waiting for another ship."

"Where's the other ship?" asked the child, looking round at the horizon that was clear.

"We can't see it yet," replied the unhappy man, "but it will come."

The long-boat and the quarter-boat were slowly approaching. They looked like beetles crawling over the water, and after them across the glittering surface came a dullness that took the sparkle from the sea—a dullness that swept and spread like an eclipse shadow.

Now the wind struck the dinghy. It was like a wind from fairyland, almost imperceptible, chill, and dimming the sun. A wind from Lilliput. As it struck the dinghy, the fog took the distant ship.

It was a most extraordinary sight, for in less than thirty seconds the ship of wood became a ship of gauze, a tracery—flickered, and was gone forever from the sight of man.

V

Voices Heard in the Mist

The sun became fainter still, and vanished. Though the air round the dinghy seemed quite clear, the on-coming boats were hazy and dim, and that part of the horizon that had been fairly clear was now blotted out.

The long-boat was leading by a good way. When she was within hailing distance the captain's voice came.

"Dinghy ahoy!"

"Ahoy!"

"Fetch alongside here!"

The long-boat ceased rowing to wait for the quarter-boat that was slowly creeping up. She was a heavy boat to pull at all times, and now she was overloaded.

The wrath of Captain Le Farge with Paddy Button for the way he had stampeded the crew was profound, but he had not time to give vent to it.

"Here, get aboard us, Mr. Lestrange!" said he, when the dinghy was alongside; "we have room for one. Mrs. Stannard is in the quarter-boat, and it's overcrowded; she's better aboard the dinghy, for she can look after the kids. Come, hurry up, the smother is coming down on us fast. Ahoy!"—to the quarter-boat—"hurry up, hurry up!"

The quarter-boat had suddenly vanished.

Mr. Lestrange climbed into the long-boat. Paddy pushed the dinghy a few yards away with the tip of a scull, and then lay on his oars waiting.

"Ahoy! ahoy!" cried Le Farge.

"Ahoy!" came from the fog bank.

Next moment the long-boat and the dinghy vanished from each other's sight: the great fog bank had taken them.

Now a couple of strokes of the port scull would have brought Mr. Button alongside the long-boat, so close was he; but the quarter-boat was in his mind, or rather imagination, so what must he do but take three powerful strokes in the direction in which he fancied the quarter-boat to be.

The rest was voices.

"Dinghy ahoy!"

"Ahoy!"

"Ahoy!"

"Don't be shoutin' together, or I'll not know which way to pull. Quarter-boat ahoy! where are yiz?"

"Port your helm!"

"Ay, ay!"—putting his helm, so to speak, to starboard—"I'll be wid yiz in wan minute—two or three minutes' hard pulling."

"Ahoy!"—much more faint.

"What d'ye mane rowin' away from me?"—a dozen strokes.

"Ahoy!"—fainter still.

Mr. Button rested on his oars.

"Divil mend them—I b'lave that was the long-boat shoutin'."

He took to his oars again and pulled vigorously.

"Paddy," came Dick's small voice, apparently from nowhere, "where are we now?"

"Sure, we're in a fog; where else would we be? Don't you be affeared."

"I ain't affeared, but Em's shivering."

"Give her me coat," said the oarsman, resting on his oars and taking it off. "Wrap it round her; and when it's round her we'll all let one big halloo together. There's an ould shawl som'er in the boat, but I can't be after lookin' for it now."

He held out the coat and an almost invisible hand took it; at the same moment a tremendous report shook the sea and sky.

"There she goes," said Mr. Button; "an' me old fiddle an' all. Don't be frightened, childer; it's only a gun they're firin' for diversion. Now we'll all halloo togither—are yiz ready?"

"Ay, ay," said Dick, who was a picker-up of sea terms.

"Halloo!" yelled Pat.

"Halloo! Halloo!" piped Dick and Emmeline.

A faint reply came, but from where, it was difficult to say. The old man rowed a few strokes and then paused on his oars. So still was the surface of the sea that the chuckling of the water at the boat's bow as she drove forward under the impetus of the last powerful stroke could be heard distinctly. It died out as she lost way, and silence closed round them like a ring.

The light from above, a light that seemed to come through a vast scuttle of deeply-muffed glass, faint though it was, almost to extinction, still varied as the little boat floated through the strata of the mist.

A great sea fog is not homogeneous—its density varies: it is honeycombed with streets, it has its caves of clear air, its cliffs of solid vapour, all shifting and changing place with the subtlety of legerdemain. It has also this wizard peculiarity, that it grows with the sinking of the sun and the approach of darkness.

The sun, could they have seen it, was now leaving the horizon.

They called again. Then they waited, but there was no response.

"There's no use bawlin' like bulls to chaps that's deaf as adders," said the old sailor, shipping his oars; immediately upon which declaration he gave another shout, with the same result as far as eliciting a reply.

"Mr. Button!" came Emmeline's voice.

"What is it, honey?"

"I'm—m—'fraid."

"You wait wan minit till I find the shawl—here it is, by the same token!—an' I'll wrap you up in it."

He crept cautiously aft to the stern-sheets and took Emmeline in his arms.

"Don't want the shawl," said Emmeline; "I'm not so much afraid in your coat." The rough, tobacco-smelling old coat gave her courage somehow.

"Well, thin, keep it on. Dicky, are you cowld?"

"I've got into daddy's great-coat; he left it behind him."

"Well, thin, I'll put the shawl round me own shoulders, for it's cowld I am. Are y' hungry, childer?"

"No," said Dick, "but I'm drefful—Hi—yow—"

"Slapy, is it? Well, down you get in the bottom of the boat, and here's the shawl for a pilla. I'll be rowin' again in a minit to keep meself warm."

He buttoned the top button of the coat.

"I'm a'right," murmured Emmeline in a dreamy voice.

"Shut your eyes tight," replied Mr. Button, "or Billy Winker will be dridgin' sand in them.

> "'Shoheen, shoheen, shoheen, shoheen,
> Sho-hu-lo, sho-hu-lo.
> Shoheen, shoheen, shoheen, shoheen,
> Hush a by the babby O.'"

It was the tag of an old nursery folk-song they sing in the hovels of the Achill coast fixed in his memory, along with the rain and the wind

HENRY DE VERE STACPOOLE

and the smell of the burning turf, and the grunting of the pig and the knickety-knock of a rocking cradle.

"She's off," murmured Mr. Button to himself, as the form in his arms relaxed. Then he laid her gently down beside Dick. He shifted forward, moving like a crab. Then he put his hand to his pocket for his pipe and tobacco and tinder box. They were in his coat pocket, but Emmeline was in his coat. To search for them would be to awaken her.

The darkness of night was now adding itself to the blindness of the fog. The oarsman could not see even the thole pins. He sat adrift mind and body. He was, to use his own expression, "moithered." Haunted by the mist, tormented by "shapes."

It was just in a fog like this that the Merrows could be heard disporting in Dunbeg bay, and off the Achill coast. Sporting and laughing, and hallooing through the mist, to lead unfortunate fishermen astray.

Merrows are not altogether evil, but they have green hair and teeth, fishes' tails and fins for arms; and to hear them walloping in the water around you like salmon, and you alone in a small boat, with the dread of one coming floundering on board, is enough to turn a man's hair grey.

For a moment he thought of awakening the children to keep him company, but he was ashamed. Then he took to the sculls again, and rowed "by the feel of the water." The creak of the oars was like a companion's voice, the exercise lulled his fears. Now and again, forgetful of the sleeping children, he gave a halloo, and paused to listen. But no answer came.

Then he continued rowing, long, steady, laborious strokes, each taking him further and further from the boats that he was never destined to sight again.

VI

Dawn on a Wide, Wide Sea

I s it aslape I've been?" said Mr. Button, suddenly awaking with a start. He had shipped his oars just for a minute's rest. He must have slept for hours, for now, behold! a warm, gentle wind was blowing, the moon was shining, and the fog was gone.

"Is it dhraming I've been?" continued the awakened one. "Where am I at all, at all? O musha! sure, here I am. O wirra! wirra! I dreamt I'd gone aslape on the main-hatch and the ship was blown up with powther, and it's all come true."

"Mr. Button!" came a small voice from the stern-sheets (Emmeline's).

"What is it, honey?"

"Where are we now?"

"Sure, we're afloat on the say, acushla; where else would we be?"

"Where's uncle?"

"He's beyant there in the long-boat—he'll be afther us in a minit."

"I want a drink."

He filled a tin pannikin that was by the beaker of water, and gave her a drink. Then he took his pipe and tobacco from his coat pocket.

She almost immediately fell asleep again beside Dick, who had not stirred or moved; and the old sailor, standing up and steadying himself, cast his eyes round the horizon. Not a sign of sail or boat was there on all the moonlit sea.

From the low elevation of an open boat one has a very small horizon, and in the vague world of moonlight somewhere round about it was possible that the boats might be near enough to show up at daybreak.

But open boats a few miles apart may be separated by long leagues in the course of a few hours. Nothing is more mysterious than the currents of the sea.

The ocean is an ocean of rivers, some swiftly flowing, some slow, and a league from where you are drifting at the rate of a mile an hour another boat may be drifting two.

A slight warm breeze was frosting the water, blending moonshine and star shimmer; the ocean lay like a lake, yet the nearest mainland was perhaps a thousand miles away.

HENRY DE VERE STACPOOLE

The thoughts of youth may be long, long thoughts, but not longer than the thoughts of this old sailor man smoking his pipe under the stars. Thoughts as long as the world is round. Blazing bar rooms in Callao—harbours over whose oily surfaces the sampans slipped like water-beetles—the lights of Macao—the docks of London. Scarcely ever a sea picture, pure and simple, for why should an old seaman care to think about the sea, where life is all into the fo'c's'le and out again, where one voyage blends and jumbles with another, where after forty-five years of reefing topsails you can't well remember off which ship it was Jack Rafferty fell overboard, or who it was killed who in the fo'c's'le of what, though you can still see, as in a mirror darkly, the fight, and the bloody face over which a man is holding a kerosene lamp.

I doubt if Paddy Button could have told you the name of the first ship he ever sailed in. If you had asked him, he would probably have replied: "I disremimber; it was to the Baltic, and cruel cowld weather, and I was say-sick—till I near brought me boots up; and it was 'O for ould Ireland!' I was cryin' all the time, an' the captin dhrummin me back with a rope's end to the tune uv it—but the name of the hooker—I disremimber—bad luck to her, whoever she was!"

So he sat smoking his pipe, whilst the candles of heaven burned above him, and calling to mind roaring drunken scenes and palm-shadowed harbours, and the men and the women he had known—such men and such women! The derelicts of the earth and the ocean. Then he nodded off to sleep again, and when he awoke the moon had gone.

Now in the eastern sky might have been seen a pale fan of light, vague as the wing of an ephemera. It vanished and changed back to darkness.

Presently, and almost at a stroke, a pencil of fire ruled a line along the eastern horizon, and the eastern sky became more beautiful than a rose leaf plucked in May. The line of fire contracted into one increasing spot, the rim of the rising sun.

As the light increased the sky above became of a blue impossible to imagine unless seen, a wan blue, yet living and sparkling as if born of the impalpable dust of sapphires. Then the whole sea flashed like the harp of Apollo touched by the fingers of the god. The light was music to the soul. It was day.

"Daddy!" suddenly cried Dick, sitting up in the sunlight and rubbing his eyes with his open palms. "Where are we?"

"All right, Dicky, me son!" cried the old sailor, who had been standing up casting his eyes round in a vain endeavour to sight the boats. "Your daddy's as safe as if he was in hivin; he'll be wid us in a minit, an' bring another ship along with him. So you're awake, are you, Em'line?"

Emmeline, sitting up in the old pilot coat, nodded in reply without speaking. Another child might have supplemented Dick's enquiries as to her uncle by questions of her own, but she did not.

Did she guess that there was some subterfuge in Mr. Button's answer, and that things were different from what he was making them out to be? Who can tell?

She was wearing an old cap of Dick's, which Mrs. Stannard in the hurry and confusion had popped on her head. It was pushed to one side, and she made a quaint enough little figure as she sat up in the early morning brightness, dressed in the old salt-stained coat beside Dick, whose straw hat was somewhere in the bottom of the boat, and whose auburn locks were blowing in the faint breeze.

"Hurroo!" cried Dick, looking around at the blue and sparkling water, and banging with a stretcher on the bottom of the boat. "I'm goin' to be a sailor, aren't I, Paddy? You'll let me sail the boat, won't you, Paddy, an' show me how to row?"

"Aisy does it," said Paddy, taking hold of the child. "I haven't a sponge or towel, but I'll just wash your face in salt wather and lave you to dry in the sun."

He filled the bailing tin with sea water.

"I don't want to wash!" shouted Dick.

"Stick your face into the water in the tin," commanded Paddy. "You wouldn't be going about the place with your face like a sut-bag, would you?"

"Stick yours in!" commanded the other.

Mr. Button did so, and made a hub-bubbling noise in the water; then he lifted a wet and streaming face, and flung the contents of the bailing tin overboard.

"Now you've lost your chance," said this arch nursery-strategist, "all the water's gone."

"There's more in the sea."

"There's no more to wash with, not till tomorrow—the fishes don't allow it."

"I want to wash," grumbled Dick. "I want to stick my face in the tin, same's you did; 'sides, Em hasn't washed."

"*I* don't mind," murmured Emmeline.

"Well, thin," said Mr. Button, as if making a sudden resolve, "I'll ax the sharks." He leaned over the boat's side, his face close to the

HENRY DE VERE STACPOOLE

surface of the water. "Halloo there!" he shouted, and then bent his head sideways to listen; the children also looked over the side, deeply interested.

"Halloo there! Are y'aslape—Oh, there y'are! Here's a spalpeen with a dhirty face, an's wishful to wash it; may I take a bailin' tin of—Oh, thank your 'arner, thank your 'arner—good day to you, and my respects."

"What did the shark say, Mr. Button?" asked Emmeline.

"He said: 'Take a bar'l full, an' welcome, Mister Button; an' it's wishful I am I had a drop of the crathur to offer you this fine marnin'.' Thin he popped his head under his fin and went aslape again; leastwise, I heard him snore."

Emmeline nearly always "Mr. Buttoned" her friend; sometimes she called him "Mr. Paddy." As for Dick, it was always "Paddy," pure and simple. Children have etiquettes of their own.

It must often strike landsmen and landswomen that the most terrible experience when cast away at sea in an open boat is the total absence of privacy. It seems an outrage on decency on the part of Providence to herd people together so. But, whoever has gone through the experience will bear me out that in great moments of life like this the human mind enlarges, and things that would shock us ashore are as nothing out there, face to face with eternity.

If so with grown-up people, how much more so with this old shell-back and his two charges?

And indeed Mr. Button was a person who called a spade a spade, had no more conventions than a walrus, and looked after his two charges just as a nursemaid might look after her charges, or a walrus after its young.

There was a large bag of biscuits in the boat, and some tinned stuff— mostly sardines.

I have known a sailor to open a box of sardines with a tin-tack. He was in prison, the sardines had been smuggled into him, and he had no can-opener. Only his genius and a tin-tack.

Paddy had a jack-knife, however, and in a marvellously short time a box of sardines was opened, and placed on the stern-sheets beside some biscuits.

These, with some water and Emmeline's Tangerine orange, which she produced and added to the common store, formed the feast, and they fell to.

When they had finished, the remains were put carefully away, and they proceeded to step the tiny mast.

The sailor, when the mast was in its place, stood for a moment resting his hand on it, and gazing around him over the vast and voiceless blue.

The Pacific has three blues: the blue of morning, the blue of midday, and the blue of evening. But the blue of morning is the happiest: the happiest thing in colour—sparkling, vague, newborn—the blue of heaven and youth.

"What are you looking for, Paddy?" asked Dick.

"Say-gulls," replied the prevaricator; then to himself: "Not a sight or a sound of them! Musha! musha! which way will I steer—north, south, aist, or west? It's all wan, for if I steer to the aist, they may be in the west; and if I steer to the west, they may be in the aist; and I can't steer to the west, for I'd be steering right in the wind's eye. Aist it is; I'll make a soldier's wind of it, and thrust to chance."

He set the sail and came aft with the sheet. Then he shifted the rudder, lit a pipe, leaned luxuriously back and gave the bellying sail to the gentle breeze.

It was part of his profession, part of his nature, that, steering, maybe, straight towards death by starvation and thirst, he was as unconcerned as if he were taking the children for a summer's sail. His imagination dealt little with the future; almost entirely influenced by his immediate surroundings, it could conjure up no fears from the scene now before it. The children were the same.

Never was there a happier starting, more joy in a little boat. During breakfast the seaman had given his charges to understand that if Dick did not meet his father and Emmeline her uncle in a "while or two," it was because he had gone on board a ship, and he'd be along presently. The terror of their position was as deeply veiled from them as eternity is veiled from you or me.

The Pacific was still bound by one of those glacial calms that can only occur when the sea has been free from storms for a vast extent of its surface, for a hurricane down by the Horn will send its swell and disturbance beyond the Marquesas. De Bois in his table of amplitudes points out that more than half the sea disturbances at any given space are caused, not by the wind, but by storms at a great distance.

But the sleep of the Pacific is only apparent. This placid lake, over which the dinghy was pursuing the running ripple, was heaving to an imperceptible swell and breaking on the shores of the Low Archipelago, and the Marquesas in foam and thunder.

Emmeline's rag-doll was a shocking affair from a hygienic or artistic standpoint. Its face was just inked on, it had no features, no arms; yet not for all the dolls in the world would she have exchanged this filthy and nearly formless thing. It was a fetish.

She sat nursing it on one side of the helmsman, whilst Dick, on the other side, hung his nose over the water, on the look-out for fish.

"Why do you smoke, Mr. Button?" asked Emmeline, who had been watching her friend for sometime in silence.

"To aise me thrubbles," replied Paddy.

He was leaning back with one eye shut and the other fixed on the luff of the sail. He was in his element: nothing to do but steer and smoke, warmed by the sun and cooled by the breeze. A landsman would have been half demented in his condition, many a sailor would have been taciturn and surly, on the look-out for sails, and alternately damning his soul and praying to his God. Paddy smoked.

"Whoop!" cried Dick. "Look, Paddy!"

An albicore a few cables lengths to port had taken a flying leap from the flashing sea, turned a complete somersault and vanished.

"It's an albicore takin' a buck lep. Hundreds I've seen before this; he's bein' chased."

"What's chasing him, Paddy?"

"What's chasin' him?—why, what else but the gibly-gobly-ums!"

Before Dick could enquire as to the personal appearance and habits of the latter, a shoal of silver arrow heads passed the boat and flittered into the water with a hissing sound.

"Thim's flyin' fish. What are you sayin'—fish can't fly! Where's the eyes in your head?"

"Are the gibblyums chasing them too?" asked Emmeline fearfully.

"No; 'tis the Billy balloos that's after thim. Don't be axin' me anymore questions now, or I'll be tellin' you lies in a minit."

Emmeline, it will be remembered, had brought a small parcel with her done up in a little shawl; it was under the boat seat, and every now and then she would stoop down to see if it were safe.

VII

Story of the Pig and the Billy-Goat

E very hour or so Mr. Button would shake his lethargy off, and rise and look round for "sea-gulls," but the prospect was sail-less as the prehistoric sea, wingless, voiceless. When Dick would fret now and then, the old sailor would always devise some means of amusing him. He made him fishing-tackle out of a bent pin and some small twine that happened to be in the boat, and told him to fish for "pinkeens"; and Dick, with the pathetic faith of childhood, fished.

Then he told them things. He had spent a year at Deal long ago, where a cousin of his was married to a boatman.

Mr. Button had put in a year as a longshoreman at Deal, and he had got a great lot to tell of his cousin and her husband, and more especially of one, Hannah; Hannah was his cousin's baby—a most marvellous child, who was born with its "buck" teeth fully developed, and whose first unnatural act on entering the world was to make a snap at the "docther." "Hung on to his fist like a bull-dog, and him bawlin' 'Murther!'"

"Mrs. James," said Emmeline, referring to a Boston acquaintance, "had a little baby, and it was pink."

"Ay, ay," said Paddy; "they're mostly pink to start with, but they fade whin they're washed."

"It'd no teeth," said Emmeline, "for I put my finger in to see."

"The doctor brought it in a bag," put in Dick, who was still steadily fishing—"dug it out of a cabbage patch; an' I got a trow'l and dug all our cabbage patch up, but there weren't any babies—but there were no end of worms."

"I wish I had a baby," said Emmeline, "and *I* wouldn't send it back to the cabbage patch."

"The doctor," explained Dick, "took it back and planted it again; and Mrs. James cried when I asked her, and daddy said it was put back to grow and turn into an angel."

"Angels have wings," said Emmeline dreamily.

"And," pursued Dick, "I told cook, and she said to Jane, daddy was always stuffing children up with—something or 'nother. And I asked

HENRY DE VERE STACPOOLE

daddy to let me see him stuffing up a child—and daddy said cook'd have to go away for saying that, and she went away next day."

"She had three big trunks and a box for her bonnet," said Emmeline, with a far-away look as she recalled the incident.

"And the cabman asked her hadn't she anymore trunks to put on his cab, and hadn't she forgot the parrot cage," said Dick.

"I wish *I* had a parrot in a cage," murmured Emmeline, moving slightly so as to get more in the shadow of the sail.

"And what in the world would you be doin' with a par't in a cage?" asked Mr. Button.

"I'd let it out," replied Emmeline.

"Spakin' about lettin' par'ts out of cages, I remimber me grandfather had an ould pig," said Paddy (they were all talking seriously together like equals). "I was a spalpeen no bigger than the height of me knee, and I'd go to the sty door, and he'd come to the door, and grunt an' blow wid his nose undher it; an' I'd grunt back to vex him, an' hammer wid me fist on it, an' shout 'Halloo there! halloo there!' and 'Halloo to you!' he'd say, spakin' the pigs' language. 'Let me out,' he'd say, 'and I'll give yiz a silver shilling.'

"'Pass it under the door,' I'd answer him. Thin he'd stick the snout of him undher the door an' I'd hit it a clip with a stick, and he'd yell murther Irish. An' me mother'd come out an' baste me, an' well I desarved it.

"Well, wan day I opened the sty door, an' out he boulted and away and beyant, over hill and hollo he goes till he gets to the edge of the cliff overlookin' the say, and there he meets a billy-goat, and he and the billy-goat has a division of opinion.

"'Away wid yiz!' says the billy-goat.

"'Away wid yourself!' says he.

"'Whose you talkin' to?' says t'other.

"'Yourself,' says him.

"'Who stole the eggs?' says the billy-goat.

"'Ax your ould grandmother!' says the pig.

"'Ax me ould *which* mother?' says the billy-goat.

"'Oh, ax me—' And before he could complete the sintence ram, blam, the ouldbilly-goat butts him in the chist, and away goes the both of thim whirtlin into the say below.

"Thin me ould grandfather comes out, and collars me by the scruff, and 'Into the sty with you!' says he; and into the sty I wint, and there they kep' me for a fortni't on bran mash and skim milk—and well I desarved it."

They dined somewhere about eleven o'clock, and at noon Paddy unstepped the mast and made a sort of little tent or awning with the sail in the bow of the boat to protect the children from the rays of the vertical sun.

Then he took his place in the bottom of the boat, in the stern, stuck Dick's straw hat over his face to preserve it from the sun, kicked about a bit to get a comfortable position, and fell asleep.

VIII

"S-H-E-N-A-N-D-O-A-H"

He had slept an hour and more when he was brought to his senses by a thin and prolonged shriek. It was Emmeline in a nightmare, or more properly a day-mare, brought on by a meal of sardines and the haunting memory of the gibbly-gobbly-ums. When she was shaken (it always took a considerable time to bring her to, from these seizures) and comforted, the mast was restepped.

As Mr. Button stood with his hand on the spar looking round him before going aft with the sheet, an object struck his eye some three miles ahead. Objects rather, for they were the masts and spars of a small ship rising from the water. Not a vestige of sail, just the naked spars. It might have been a couple of old skeleton trees jutting out of the water for all a landsman could have told.

He stared at this sight for twenty or thirty seconds without speaking, his head projected like the head of a tortoise. Then he gave a wild "Hurroo!"

"What is it, Paddy?" asked Dick.

"Hurroo!" replied Mr. Button. "Ship ahoy! ship ahoy! Lie to till I be afther boardin' you. Sure, they are lyin' to—divil a rag of canvas on her—are they aslape or dhramin'? Here, Dick, let me get aft wid the sheet; the wind'll take us up to her quicker than we'll row."

He crawled aft and took the tiller; the breeze took the sail, and the boat forged ahead.

"Is it daddy's ship?" asked Dick, who was almost as excited as his friend.

"I dinno; we'll see when we fetch her."

"Shall we go on her, Mr. Button?" asked Emmeline.

"Ay will we, honey."

Emmeline bent down, and fetching her parcel from under the seat, held it in her lap.

As they drew nearer, the outlines of the ship became more apparent. She was a small brig, with stump topmasts, from the spars a few rags of canvas fluttered. It was apparent soon to the old sailor's eye what was amiss with her.

"She's derelick, bad cess to her!" he muttered; "derelick and done for—just me luck!"

"I can't see any people on the ship," cried Dick, who had crept forward to the bow. "Daddy's not there."

The old sailor let the boat off a point or two, so as to get a view of the brig more fully; when they were within twenty cable lengths or so he unstepped the mast and took to the sculls.

The little brig floated very low on the water, and presented a mournful enough appearance; her running rigging all slack, shreds of canvas flapping at the yards, and no boats hanging at her davits. It was easy enough to see that she was a timber ship, and that she had started a butt, flooded herself and been abandoned.

Paddy lay on his oars within a few strokes of her. She was floating as placidly as though she were in the harbour of San Francisco; the green water showed in her shadow, and in the green water waved the tropic weeds that were growing from her copper. Her paint was blistered and burnt absolutely as though a hot iron had been passed over it, and over her taffrail hung a large rope whose end was lost to sight in the water.

A few strokes brought them under the stern. The name of the ship was there in faded letters, also the port to which she belonged. "*Shenandoah*. Martha's Vineyard."

"There's letters on her," said Mr. Button. "But I can't make thim out. I've no larnin'."

"I can read them," said Dick.

"So c'n I," murmured Emmeline.

"S-H-E-N-A-N-D-O-A-H," spelt Dick.

"What's that?" enquired Paddy.

"I don't know," replied Dick, rather downcastedly.

"There you are!" cried the oarsman in a disgusted manner, pulling the boat round to the starboard side of the brig. "They pritind to tache letters to childer in schools, pickin' their eyes out wid book-readin', and here's letters as big as me face an' they can't make hid or tail of them— be dashed to book-readin'!"

The brig had old-fashioned wide channels, regular platforms; and she floated so low in the water that they were scarcely a foot above the level of the dinghy.

Mr. Button secured the boat by passing the painter through a channel plate, then, with Emmeline and her parcel in his arms or rather in one arm, he clambered over the channel and passed her over the rail

HENRY DE VERE STACPOOLE

on to the deck. Then it was Dick's turn, and the children stood waiting whilst the old sailor brought the beaker of water, the biscuit, and the tinned stuff on board.

It was a place to delight the heart of a boy, the deck of the *Shenandoah*; forward right from the main hatchway it was laden with timber. Running rigging lay loose on the deck in coils, and nearly the whole of the quarter-deck was occupied by a deck-house. The place had a delightful smell of sea-beach, decaying wood, tar, and mystery. Bights of buntline and other ropes were dangling from above, only waiting to be swung from. A bell was hung just forward of the foremast. In half a moment Dick was forward hammering at the bell with a belaying pin he had picked from the deck.

Mr. Button shouted to him to desist; the sound of the bell jarred on his nerves. It sounded like a summons, and a summons on that deserted craft was quite out of place. Who knew what mightn't answer it in the way of the supernatural?

Dick dropped the belaying pin and ran forward. He took the disengaged hand, and the three went aft to the door of the deck-house. The door was open, and they peeped in.

The place had three windows on the starboard side, and through the windows the sun was shining in a mournful manner. There was a table in the middle of the place. A seat was pushed away from the table as if someone had risen in a hurry. On the table lay the remains of a meal, a teapot, two teacups, two plates. On one of the plates rested a fork with a bit of putrifying bacon upon it that someone had evidently been conveying to his mouth when—something had happened. Near the teapot stood a tin of condensed milk, haggled open. Some old salt had just been in the act of putting milk in his tea when the mysterious something had occurred. Never did a lot of dead things speak so eloquently as these things spoke.

One could conjure it all up. The skipper, most likely, had finished his tea, and the mate was hard at work at his, when the leak had been discovered, or some derelict had been run into, or whatever it was had happened—happened.

One thing was evident, that since the abandonment of the brig she had experienced fine weather, else the things would not have been left standing so trimly on the table.

Mr. Button and Dick entered the place to prosecute enquiries, but Emmeline remained at the door. The charm of the old brig appealed to her almost as much as to Dick, but she had a feeling about it quite unknown to him. A ship where no one was had about it suggestions of "other things."

She was afraid to enter the gloomy deck-house, and afraid to remain alone outside; she compromised matters by sitting down on the deck. Then she placed the small bundle beside her, and hurriedly took the rag-doll from her pocket, into which it was stuffed head down, pulled its calico skirt from over its head, propped it up against the coaming of the door, and told it not to be afraid.

There was not much to be found in the deck-house, but aft of it were two small cabins like rabbit hutches, once inhabited by the skipper and his mate. Here there were great findings in the way of rubbish. Old clothes, old boots, an old top-hat of that extraordinary pattern you may see in the streets of Pernambuco, immensely tall, and narrowing towards the brim. A telescope without a lens, a volume of Hoyt, a nautical almanac, a great bolt of striped flannel shirting, a box of fish hooks. And in one corner—glorious find!—a coil of what seemed to be ten yards or so of black rope.

"Baccy, begorra!" shouted Pat, seizing upon his treasure. It was pigtail. You may see coils of it in the tobacconists' windows of seaport towns. A pipe full of it would make a hippopotamus vomit, yet old sailors chew it and smoke it and revel in it.

"We'll bring all the lot of the things out on deck, and see what's worth keepin' an' what's worth leavin'," said Mr. Button, taking an immense armful of the old truck; whilst Dick, carrying the top-hat, upon which he had instantly seized as his own special booty, led the way.

"Em," shouted Dick, as he emerged from the doorway, "see what I've got!"

He popped the awful-looking structure over his head. It went right down to his shoulders.

Emmeline gave a shriek.

"It smells funny," said Dick, taking it off and applying his nose to the inside of it—"smells like an old hair brush. Here, you try it on."

Emmeline scrambled away as far as she could, till she reached the starboard bulwarks, where she sat in the scupper, breathless and speechless and wide-eyed. She was always dumb when frightened (unless it were a nightmare or a very sudden shock), and this hat suddenly seen half covering Dick frightened her out of her wits. Besides, it was a black thing, and she hated black things—black cats, black horses; worst of all, black dogs.

She had once seen a hearse in the streets of Boston, an old-time hearse with black plumes, trappings and all complete. The sight had nearly given her a fit, though she did not know in the least the meaning of it.

Meanwhile Mr. Button was conveying armful after armful of stuff on deck. When the heap was complete, he sat down beside it in the glorious afternoon sunshine, and lit his pipe.

He had searched neither for food or water as yet; content with the treasure God had given him, for the moment the material things of life were forgotten. And, indeed, if he had searched he would have found only half a sack of potatoes in the caboose, for the lazarette was awash, and the water in the scuttle-butt was stinking.

Emmeline, seeing what was in progress, crept up, Dick promising not to put the hat on her, and they all sat round the pile.

"Thim pair of brogues," said the old man, holding a pair of old boots up for inspection like an auctioneer, "would fetch half a dollar any day in the wake in any sayport in the world. Put them beside you, Dick, and lay hold of this pair of britches by the ends of em'—stritch them."

The trousers were stretched out, examined and approved of, and laid beside the boots.

"Here's a tiliscope wid wan eye shut," said Mr. Button, examining the broken telescope and pulling it in and out like a concertina. "Stick it beside the brogues; it may come in handy for somethin'. Here's a book"—tossing the nautical almanac to the boy. "Tell me what it says."

Dick examined the pages of figures hopelessly.

"I can't read 'em," said Dick; "it's numbers."

"Buzz it overboard," said Mr. Button.

Dick did what he was told joyfully, and the proceedings resumed.

He tried on the tall hat, and the children laughed. On her old friend's head the thing ceased to have terror for Emmeline.

She had two methods of laughing. The angelic smile before mentioned—a rare thing—and, almost as rare, a laugh in which she showed her little white teeth, whilst she pressed her hands together, the left one tight shut, and the right clasped over it.

He put the hat on one side, and continued the sorting, searching all the pockets of the clothes and finding nothing. When he had arranged what to keep, they flung the rest overboard, and the valuables were conveyed to the captain's cabin, there to remain till wanted.

Then the idea that food might turn up useful as well as old clothes in their present condition struck the imaginative mind of Mr. Button, and he proceeded to search.

The lazarette was simply a cistern full of sea water; what else it might contain, not being a diver, he could not say. In the copper of the caboose lay a great lump of putrifying pork or meat of some sort. The harness cask contained nothing except huge crystals of salt. All the meat had been taken away. Still, the provisions and water brought on board from the dinghy would be sufficient to last them some ten days or so, and in the course of ten days a lot of things might happen.

Mr. Button leaned over the side. The dinghy was nestling beside the brig like a duckling beside a duck; the broad channel might have been likened to the duck's wing half extended. He got on the channel to see if the painter was safely attached. Having made all secure, he climbed slowly up to the main-yard arm, and looked round upon the sea.

IX

Shadows in the Moonlight

Daddy's a long time coming," said Dick all of a sudden.

They were seated on the baulks of timber that cumbered the deck of the brig on either side of the caboose. An ideal perch. The sun was setting over Australia way, in a sea that seemed like a sea of boiling gold. Some mystery of mirage caused the water to heave and tremble as if troubled by fervent heat.

"Ay, is he," said Mr. Button; "but it's better late than never. Now don't be thinkin' of him, for that won't bring him. Look at the sun goin' into the wather, and don't be spakin' a word, now, but listen and you'll hear it hiss."

The children gazed and listened, Paddy also. All three were mute as the great blazing shield touched the water that leapt to meet it.

You *could* hear the water hiss—if you had imagination enough. Once having touched the water, the sun went down behind it, as swiftly as a man in a hurry going down a ladder. As he vanished a ghostly and golden twilight spread over the sea, a light exquisite but immensely forlorn. Then the sea became a violet shadow, the west darkened as if to a closing door, and the stars rushed over the sky.

"Mr. Button," said Emmeline, nodding towards the sun as he vanished, "where's over there?"

"The west," replied he, staring at the sunset. "Chainy and Injee and all away beyant."

"Where's the sun gone to now, Paddy?" asked Dick.

"He's gone chasin' the moon, an' she's skedadlin' wid her dress brailed up for all she's worth; she'll be along up in a minit. He's always afther her, but he's never caught her yet."

"What would he do to her if he caught her?" asked Emmeline.

"Faith, an' maybe he'd fetch her a skelp—an' well she'd desarve it."

"Why'd she deserve it?" asked Dick, who was in one of his questioning moods.

"Because she's always delutherin' people an' leadin' thim asthray. Girls or men, she moidhers thim all once she gets the comeither on them; same as she did Buck M'Cann."

"Who's he?"

"Buck M'Cann? Faith, he was the village ijit where I used to live in the ould days."

"What's that?"

"Hould your whisht, an' don't be axin' questions. He was always wantin' the moon, though he was twinty an' six feet four. He'd a gob on him that hung open like a rat-trap with a broken spring, and he was as thin as a barber's pole, you could a' tied a reef knot in the middle of 'um; and whin the moon was full there was no houldin' him." Mr. Button gazed at the reflection of the sunset on the water for a moment as if recalling some form from the past, and then proceeded. "He'd sit on the grass starin' at her, an' thin he'd start to chase her over the hills, and they'd find him at last, maybe a day or two later, lost in the mountains, grazin' on berries, an' as green as a cabbidge from the hunger an' the cowld, till it got so bad at long last they had to hobble him."

"I've seen a donkey hobbled," cried Dick.

"Thin you've seen the twin brother of Buck M'Cann. Well, one night me elder brother Tim was sittin' over the fire, smokin' his dudeen an' thinkin' of his sins, when in comes Buck with the hobbles on him.

"'Tim,' says he, 'I've got her at last!'

"'Got who?' says Tim.

"'The moon,' says he.

"'Got her where?' says Tim.

"'In a bucket down by the pond,' says t'other, 'safe an' sound an' not a scratch on her; you come and look,' says he. So Tim follows him, he hobblin', and they goes to the pond side, and there, sure enough, stood a tin bucket full of wather, an' on the wather the refliction of the moon.

"'I dridged her out of the pond,' whispers Buck. 'Aisy now,' says he, 'an' I'll dribble the water out gently,' says he, 'an' we'll catch her alive at the bottom of it like a trout.' So he drains the wather out gently of the bucket till it was near all gone, an' then he looks into the bucket expectin' to find the moon flounderin' in the bottom of it like a flat fish.

"'She's gone, bad 'cess to her!' says he.

"'Try again,' says me brother, and Buck fills the bucket again, and there was the moon sure enough when the water came to stand still.

"'Go on,' says me brother. 'Drain out the wather, but go gentle, or she'll give yiz the slip again.'

"'Wan minit,' says Buck, 'I've got an idea,' says he; 'she won't give me the slip this time,' says he. 'You wait for me,' says he; and off he hobbles to his old mother's cabin a stone's-throw away, and back he comes with a sieve.

"'You hold the sieve,' says Buck, 'and I'll drain the water into it; if she 'scapes from the bucket we'll have her in the sieve.' And he pours the wather out of the bucket as gentle as if it was crame out of a jug. When all the wather was out he turns the bucket bottom up, and shook it.

"'Ran dan the thing!' he cries, 'she's gone again;' an' wid that he flings the bucket into the pond, and the sieve afther the bucket, when up comes his old mother hobbling on her stick.

"'Where's me bucket?' says she.

"'In the pond,' say Buck.

"'And me sieve?' says she.

"'Gone afther the bucket.'

"'I'll give yiz a bucketin'!' says she; and she up with the stick and landed him a skelp, an' driv him roarin' and hobblin' before her, and locked him up in the cabin, an' kep' him on bread an' wather for a wake to get the moon out of his head; but she might have saved her thruble, for that day month in it was agin—There she comes!"

The moon, argent and splendid, was breaking from the water. She was full, and her light was powerful almost as the light of day. The shadows of the children and the queer shadow of Mr. Button were cast on the wall of the caboose hard and black as silhouettes.

"Look at our shadows!" cried Dick, taking off his broad-brimmed straw hat and waving it.

Emmeline held up her doll to see *its* shadow, and Mr. Button held up his pipe.

"Come now," said he, putting the pipe back in his mouth, and making to rise, "and shadda off to bed; it's time you were aslape, the both of you."

Dick began to yowl.

"*I* don't want to go to bed; I aint tired, Paddy—les's stay a little longer."

"Not a minit," said the other, with all the decision of a nurse; "not a minit afther me pipe's out!"

"Fill it again," said Dick.

Mr. Button made no reply. The pipe gurgled as he puffed at it—a kind of death-rattle speaking of almost immediate extinction.

"Mr. Button!" said Emmeline. She was holding her nose in the air and sniffing; seated to windward of the smoker, and out of the pigtail-poisoned air, her delicate sense of smell perceived something lost to the others.

"What is it, acushla?"

"I smell something."

"What d'ye say you smell?"

"Something nice."

"What's it like?" asked Dick, sniffing hard. "*I* don't smell anything."

Emmeline sniffed again to make sure.

"Flowers," said she.

The breeze, which had shifted several points since midday, was bearing with it a faint, faint odour: a perfume of vanilla and spice so faint as to be imperceptible to all but the most acute olfactory sense.

"Flowers!" said the old sailor, tapping the ashes out of his pipe against the heel of his boot. "And where'd you get flowers in middle of the say? It's dhramin' you are. Come now—to bed widyiz!"

"Fill it again," wailed Dick, referring to the pipe.

"It's a spankin' I'll give you," replied his guardian, lifting him down from the timber baulks, and then assisting Emmeline, "in two ticks if you don't behave. Come along, Em'line."

He started aft, a small hand in each of his, Dick bellowing.

As they passed the ship's bell, Dick stretched towards the belaying pin that was still lying on the deck, seized it, and hit the bell a mighty bang. It was the last pleasure to be snatched before sleep, and he snatched it.

Paddy had made up beds for himself and his charges in the deckhouse; he had cleared the stuff off the table, broken open the windows to get the musty smell away, and placed the mattresses from the captain and mate's cabins on the floor.

When the children were in bed and asleep, he went to the starboard rail, and, leaning on it, looked over the moonlit sea. He was thinking of ships as his wandering eye roved over the sea spaces, little dreaming of the message that the perfumed breeze was bearing him. The message that had been received and dimly understood by Emmeline. Then he leaned with his back to the rail and his hands in his pockets. He was not thinking now, he was ruminating.

The basis of the Irish character as exemplified by Paddy Button is a profound laziness mixed with a profound melancholy. Yet Paddy, in his left-handed way, was as hard a worker as any man on board ship; and as for melancholy, he was the life and soul of the fo'cs'le. Yet there they were, the laziness and the melancholy, only waiting to be tapped.

As he stood with his hands thrust deep in his pockets, longshore fashion, counting the dowels in the planking of the deck by the moonlight, he was reviewing the "old days." The tale of Buck M'Cann had recalled them, and across all the salt seas he could see the moonlight on the Connemara mountains, and hear the sea-gulls crying on the thunderous beach where each wave has behind it three thousand miles of sea.

Suddenly Mr. Button came back from the mountains of Connemara to find himself on the deck of the *Shenandoah*; and he instantly became possessed by fears. Beyond the white deserted deck, barred by the shadows of the standing rigging, he could see the door of the caboose. Suppose he should suddenly see a head pop out—or, worse, a shadowy form go in?

He turned to the deck-house, where the children were sound asleep, and where, in a few minutes, he, too, was sound asleep beside them, whilst all night long the brig rocked to the gentle swell of the Pacific, and the breeze blew, bringing with it the perfume of flowers.

X

The Tragedy of the Boats

When the fog lifted after midnight the people in the long-boat saw the quarter-boat half a mile to starboard of them.

"Can you see the dinghy?" asked Lestrange of the captain, who was standing up searching the horizon.

"Not a speck," answered Le Farge. "Damn that Irishman! but for him I'd have got the boats away properly victualled and all; as it is I don't know what we've got aboard. You, Jenkins, what have you got forward there?"

"Two bags of bread and a breaker of water," answered the steward.

"A breaker of water be sugared!" came another voice; "a breaker half full, you mean."

Then the steward's voice: "So it is; there's not more than a couple of gallons in her."

"My God!" said Le Farge. "*Damn* that Irishman!"

"There's not more than'll give us two half pannikins apiece all round," said the steward.

"Maybe," said Le Farge, "the quarter-boat's better stocked; pull for her."

"She's pulling for us," said the stroke oar.

"Captain," asked Lestrange, "are you sure there's no sight of the dinghy?"

"None," replied Le Farge.

The unfortunate man's head sank on his breast. He had little time to brood over his troubles, however, for a tragedy was beginning to unfold around him, the most shocking, perhaps, in the annals of the sea—a tragedy to be hinted at rather than spoken of.

When the boats were within hailing distance, a man in the bow of the long-boat rose up.

"Quarter-boat ahoy!"

"Ahoy!"

"How much water have you?"

"None!"

The word came floating over the placid moonlit water. At it the fellows in the long-boat ceased rowing, and you could see the water-drops dripping off their oars like diamonds in the moonlight.

HENRY DE VERE STACPOOLE

"Quarter-boat ahoy!" shouted the fellow in the bow. "Lay on your oars."

"Here, you scowbanker!" cried Le Farge, "who are you to be giving directions—"

"Scowbanker yourself!" replied the fellow. "Bullies, put her about!"

The starboard oars backed water, and the boat came round.

By chance the worst lot of the *Northumberland's* crew were in the long-boat—veritable "scowbankers," scum; and how scum clings to life you will never know, until you have been amongst it in an open boat at sea. Le Farge had no more command over this lot than you have who are reading this book.

"Heave to!" came from the quarter-boat, as she laboured behind.

"Lay on your oars, bullies!" cried the ruffian at the bow, who was still standing up like an evil genius who had taken momentary command over events. "Lay on your oars, bullies; they'd better have it now."

The quarter-boat in her turn ceased rowing, and lay a cable's length away.

"How much water have you?" came the mate's voice.

"Not enough to go round."

Le Farge made to rise, and the stroke oar struck at him, catching him in the wind and doubling him up in the bottom of the boat.

"Give us some, for God's sake!" came the mate's voice; "we're parched with rowing, and there's a woman on board."

The fellow in the bow of the long-boat, as if someone had suddenly struck him, broke into a tornado of blasphemy.

"Give us some," came the mate's voice, "or, by God, we'll lay you aboard!"

Before the words were well spoken the men in the quarter-boat carried the threat into action. The conflict was brief: the quarter-boat was too crowded for fighting. The starboard men in the long-boat fought with their oars, whilst the fellows to port steadied the boat.

The fight did not last long, and presently the quarter-boat sheered off, half of the men in her cut about the head and bleeding—two of them senseless.

IT WAS SUNDOWN ON THE following day. The long-boat lay adrift. The last drop of water had been served out eight hours before.

The quarter-boat, like a horrible phantom, had been haunting and pursuing her all day, begging for water when there was none. It was like the prayers one might expect to hear in hell.

The men in the long-boat, gloomy and morose, weighed down with a sense of crime, tortured by thirst, and tormented by the voices imploring for water, lay on their oars when the other boat tried to approach.

Now and then, suddenly, and as if moved by a common impulse, they would all shout out together: "We have none." But the quarter-boat would not believe. It was in vain to hold the breaker with the bung out to prove its dryness, the half-delirious creatures had it fixed in their minds that their comrades were withholding from them the water that was not.

Just as the sun touched the sea, Lestrange, rousing himself from a torpor into which he had sunk, raised himself and looked over the gunwale. He saw the quarter-boat drifting a cable's length away, lit by the full light of sunset, and the spectres in it, seeing him, held out in mute appeal their blackened tongues.

OF THE NIGHT THAT FOLLOWED it is almost impossible to speak. Thirst was nothing to what the scowbankers suffered from the torture of the whimpering appeal for water that came to them at intervals during the night.

WHEN AT LAST THE *ARAGO*, a French whale ship, sighted them, the crew of the long-boat were still alive, but three of them were raving madmen. Of the crew of the quarter-boat was saved—not one.

HENRY DE VERE STACPOOLE

PART II

XI

THE ISLAND

"Childer!" shouted Paddy. He was at the cross-trees in the full dawn, whilst the children standing beneath on deck were craning their faces up to him. "There's an island forenint us."

"Hurrah!" cried Dick. He was not quite sure what an island might be like in the concrete, but it was something fresh, and Paddy's voice was jubilant.

"Land ho! it is," said he, coming down to the deck. "Come for'ard to the bows, and I'll show it you."

He stood on the timber in the bows and lifted Emmeline up in his arms; and even at that humble elevation from the water she could see something of an undecided colour—green for choice—on the horizon.

It was not directly ahead, but on the starboard bow—or, as she would have expressed it, to the right. When Dick had looked and expressed his disappointment at there being so little to see, Paddy began to make preparations for leaving the ship.

It was only just now, with land in sight, that he recognised in some fashion the horror of the position from which they were about to escape.

He fed the children hurriedly with some biscuits and tinned meat, and then, with a biscuit in his hand, eating as he went, he trotted about the decks, collecting things and stowing them in the dinghy. The bolt of striped flannel, all the old clothes, a housewife full of needles and thread, such as seamen sometimes carry, the half-sack of potatoes, a saw which he found in the caboose, the precious coil of tobacco, and a lot of other odds and ends he transhipped, sinking the little dinghy several strakes in the process. Also, of course, he took the breaker of water, and the remains of the biscuit and tinned stuff they had brought on board. These being stowed, and the dinghy ready, he went forward with the children to the bow, to see how the island was bearing.

It had loomed up nearer during the hour or so in which he had been collecting and storing the things—nearer, and more to the right, which meant that the brig was being borne by a fairly swift current, and that she would pass it, leaving it two or three miles to starboard. It was well they had command of the dinghy.

"The sea's all round it," said Emmeline, who was seated on Paddy's shoulder, holding on tight to him, and gazing upon the island, the green of whose trees was now visible, an oasis of verdure in the sparkling and seraphic blue.

"Are we going there, Paddy?" asked Dick, holding on to a stay, and straining his eyes towards the land.

"Ay, are we," said Mr. Button. "Hot foot—five knots, if we're makin' wan; and it's ashore we'll be by noon, and maybe sooner."

The breeze had freshened up, and was blowing dead from the island, as though the island were making a weak attempt to blow them away from it.

Oh, what a fresh and perfumed breeze it was! All sorts of tropical growing things had joined their scent in one bouquet.

"Smell it," said Emmeline, expanding her small nostrils. "That's what I smelt last night, only it's stronger now."

The last reckoning taken on board the *Northumberland* had proved the ship to be south by east of the Marquesas; this was evidently one of those small, lost islands that lie here and there south by east of the Marquesas. Islands the most lonely and beautiful in the world.

As they gazed it grew before them, and shifted still more to the right. It was hilly and green now, though the trees could not be clearly made out; here, the green was lighter in colour, and there, darker. A rim of pure white marble seemed to surround its base. It was foam breaking on the barrier reef.

In another hour the feathery foliage of the cocoa-nut palms could be made out, and the old sailor judged it time to take to the boat.

He lifted Emmeline, who was clasping her luggage, over the rail on to the channel, and deposited her in the stern-sheets; then Dick.

In a moment the boat was adrift, the mast stepped, and the *Shenandoah* left to pursue her mysterious voyage at the will of the currents of the sea.

"You're not going to the island, Paddy," cried Dick, as the old man put the boat on the port tack.

"You be aisy," replied the other, "and don't be larnin' your gran'mother. How the divil d'ye think I'd fetch the land sailin' dead in the wind's eye?"

"Has the wind eyes?"

Mr. Button did not answer the question. He was troubled in his mind. What if the island were inhabited? He had spent several years in the South Seas. He knew the people of the Marquesas and Samoa, and liked them. But here he was out of his bearings.

However, all the troubling in the world was of no use. It was a case of the island or the deep sea, and, putting the boat on the starboard tack, he lit his pipe and leaned back with the tiller in the crook of his arm. His keen eyes had made out from the deck of the brig an opening in the reef, and he was making to run the dinghy abreast of the opening, and then take to the sculls and row her through.

Now, as they drew nearer a sound came on the breeze, a sound faint and sonorous and dreamy. It was the sound of the breakers on the reef. The sea just here was heaving to a deeper swell, as if vexed in its sleep at the resistance to it of the land.

Emmeline, sitting with her bundle in her lap, stared without speaking at the sight before her. Even in the bright, glorious sunshine, and despite the greenery that showed beyond, it was a desolate sight seen from her place in the dinghy. A white, forlorn beach, over which the breakers raced and tumbled, sea-gulls wheeling and screaming, and over all the thunder of the surf.

Suddenly the break became visible, and a glimpse of smooth, blue water beyond. Mr. Button unshipped the tiller, unstepped the mast, and took to the sculls.

As they drew nearer, the sea became more active, savage, and alive; the thunder of the surf became louder, the breakers more fierce and threatening, the opening broader.

One could see the water swirling round the coral piers, for the tide was flooding into the lagoon; it had seized the little dinghy and was bearing it along far swifter than the sculls could have driven it. Sea-gulls screamed around them, the boat rocked and swayed. Dick shouted with excitement, and Emmeline shut her eyes *tight*.

Then, as though a door had been swiftly and silently closed, the sound of the surf became suddenly less. The boat floated on an even keel; she opened her eyes and found herself in Wonderland.

XII

The Lake of Azure

On either side lay a great sweep of waving blue water. Calm, almost as a lake, sapphire here, and here with the tints of the aqua marine. Water so clear that fathoms away below you could see the branching coral, the schools of passing fish, and the shadows of the fish upon the spaces of sand.

Before them the clear water washed the sands of a white beach, the cocoa-palms waved and whispered in the breeze; and as the oarsman lay on his oars to look a flock of bluebirds rose, as if suddenly freed from the tree-tops, wheeled, and passed soundless, like a wreath of smoke, over the tree-tops of the higher land beyond.

"Look!" shouted Dick, who had his nose over the gunwale of the boat. "Look at the *fish*!"

"Mr. Button," cried Emmeline, "where are we?"

"Bedad, I dunno; but we might be in a worse place, I'm thinkin'," replied the old man, sweeping his eyes over the blue and tranquil lagoon, from the barrier reef to the happy shore.

On either side of the broad beach before them the cocoa-nut trees came down like two regiments, and bending gazed at their own reflections in the lagoon. Beyond lay waving chapparel, where cocoa-palms and breadfruit trees intermixed with the mammee apple and the tendrils of the wild vine. On one of the piers of coral at the break of the reef stood a single cocoa-palm; bending with a slight curve, it, too, seemed seeking its reflection in the waving water.

But the soul of it all, the indescribable thing about this picture of mirrored palm trees, blue lagoon, coral reef and sky, was the light.

Away at sea the light was blinding, dazzling, cruel. Away at sea it had nothing to focus itself upon, nothing to exhibit but infinite spaces of blue water and desolation.

Here it made the air a crystal, through which the gazer saw the loveliness of the land and reef, the green of palm, the white of coral, the wheeling gulls, the blue lagoon, all sharply outlined—burning, coloured, arrogant, yet tender—heart-breakingly beautiful, for the spirit of eternal morning was here, eternal happiness, eternal youth.

HENRY DE VERE STACPOOLE

As the oarsman pulled the tiny craft towards the beach, neither he nor the children saw away behind the boat, on the water near the bending palm tree at the break in the reef, something that for a moment insulted the day, and was gone. Something like a small triangle of dark canvas, that rippled through the water and sank from sight; something that appeared and vanished like an evil thought.

It did not take long to beach the boat. Mr. Button tumbled over the side up to his knees in water, whilst Dick crawled over the bow.

"Catch hould of her the same as I do," cried Paddy, laying hold of the starboard gunwale; whilst Dick, imitative as a monkey, seized the gunwale to port. Now then:

> *"Yeo ho, Chilliman,*
> *Up wid her, up wid her,*
> *Heave O, Chilliman.'*

"Lave her be now; she's high enough."

He took Emmeline in his arms and carried her up on the sand. It was from just here on the sand that you could see the true beauty of the lagoon. That lake of sea water forever protected from storm and trouble by the barrier reef of coral.

Right from where the little clear ripples ran up the strand, it led the eye to the break in the coral reef where the palm gazed at its own reflection in the water, and there, beyond the break, one caught a vision of the great heaving, sparkling sea.

The lagoon, just here, was perhaps more than a third of a mile broad. I have never measured it, but I know that, standing by the palm tree on the reef, flinging up one's arm and shouting to a person on the beach, the sound took a perceptible time to cross the water: I should say, perhaps, an almost perceptible time. The distant signal and the distant call were almost coincident, yet not quite.

Dick, mad with delight at the place in which he found himself, was running about like a dog just out of the water. Mr. Button was discharging the cargo of the dinghy on the dry, white sand. Emmeline seated herself with her precious bundle on the sand, and was watching the operations of her friend, looking at the things around her and feeling very strange.

For all she knew all this was the ordinary accompaniment of a sea voyage. Paddy's manner throughout had been set to the one idea, not to frighten the "childer"; the weather had backed him up. But down in the heart of her lay the knowledge that all was not as it should be. The hurried departure from the ship, the fog in which her uncle had vanished, those things, and others as well, she felt instinctively were not right. But she said nothing.

She had not long for meditation, however, for Dick was running towards her with a live crab which he had picked up, calling out that he was going to make it bite her.

"Take it away!" cried Emmeline, holding both hands with fingers widespread in front of her face. "Mr. Button! Mr. Button! Mr. Button!"

"Lave her be, you little divil!" roared Pat, who was depositing the last of the cargo on the sand. "Lave her be, or it's a cow-hidin' I'll be givin' you!"

"What's a 'divil,' Paddy?" asked Dick, panting from his exertions. "Paddy, what's a 'divil'?"

"You're wan. Ax no questions now, for it's tired I am, an' I want to rest me bones."

He flung himself under the shade of a palm tree, took out his tinder box, tobacco and pipe, cut some tobacco up, filled his pipe and lit it. Emmeline crawled up, and sat near him, and Dick flung himself down on the sand near Emmeline.

Mr. Button took off his coat and made a pillow of it against a cocoa-nut tree stem. He had found the El Dorado of the weary. With his knowledge of the South Seas a glance at the vegetation to be seen told him that food for a regiment might be had for the taking; water, too.

Right down the middle of the strand was a depression which in the rainy season would be the bed of a rushing rivulet. The water just now was not strong enough to come all the way to the lagoon, but away up there "beyant" in the woods lay the source, and he'd find it in due time. There was enough in the breaker for a week, and green "cuca-nuts" were to be had for the climbing.

Emmeline contemplated Paddy for a while as he smoked and rested his bones, then a great thought occurred to her. She took the little shawl from around the parcel she was holding and exposed the mysterious box.

"Oh, begorra, the box!" said Paddy, leaning on his elbow interestedly; "I might a' known you wouldn't a' forgot it."

"Mrs. James," said Emmeline, "made me promise not to open it till I got on shore, for the things in it might get lost."

"Well, you're ashore now," said Dick; "open it."

HENRY DE VERE STACPOOLE

"I'm going to," said Emmeline.

She carefully undid the string, refusing the assistance of Paddy's knife. Then the brown paper came off, disclosing a common cardboard box. She raised the lid half an inch, peeped in, and shut it again.

"*Open* it!" cried Dick, mad with curiosity.

"What's in it, honey?" asked the old sailor, who was as interested as Dick.

"Things," replied Emmeline.

Then all at once she took the lid off and disclosed a tiny tea service of china, packed in shavings; there was a teapot with a lid, a cream jug, cups and saucers, and six microscopic plates, each painted with a pansy.

"Sure, it's a tay-set!" said Paddy, in an interested voice. "Glory be to God! will you look at the little plates wid the flowers on thim?"

"Heugh!" said Dick in disgust; "I thought it might a' been soldiers."

"*I* don't want soldiers," replied Emmeline, in a voice of perfect contentment.

She unfolded a piece of tissue paper, and took from it a sugar-tongs and six spoons. Then she arrayed the whole lot on the sand.

"Well, if that don't beat all!" said Paddy.

"And whin are you goin' to ax me to tay with you?"

"Sometime," replied Emmeline, collecting the things, and carefully repacking them.

Mr. Button finished his pipe, tapped the ashes out, and placed it in his pocket.

"I'll be afther riggin' up a bit of a tint," said he, as he rose to his feet, "to shelter us from the jew tonight; but I'll first have a look at the woods to see if I can find wather. Lave your box with the other things, Emmeline; there's no one here to take it."

Emmeline left her box on the heap of things that Paddy had placed in the shadow of the cocoa-nut trees, took his hand, and the three entered the grove on the right.

It was like entering a pine forest; the tall symmetrical stems of the trees seemed set by mathematical law, each at a given distance from the other. Whichever way you entered a twilight alley set with tree boles lay before you. Looking up you saw at an immense distance above a pale green roof patined with sparkling and flashing points of light, where the breeze was busy playing with the green fronds of the trees.

"Mr. Button," murmured Emmeline, "we won't get lost, will we?"

"Lost! No, faith; sure we're goin' uphill, an' all we have to do is to come down again, when we want to get back—ware nuts!" A green nut detached from up above came down rattling and tumbling and hopped on the ground. Paddy picked it up. "It's a green cucanut," said he, putting it in his pocket (it was not very much bigger than a Jaffa orange), "and we'll have it for tay."

"That's not a cocoa-nut," said Dick; "cocoa-nuts are brown. I had five cents once an' I bought one, and scraped it out and y'et it."

"When Dr. Sims made Dicky sick," said Emmeline, "he said the wonder t'im was how Dicky held it all."

"Come on," said Mr. Button, "an' don't be talkin', or it's the Cluricaunes will be after us."

"What's cluricaunes?" demanded Dick.

"Little men no bigger than your thumb that make the brogues for the Good People."

"Who's they?"

"Whisht, and don't be talkin'. Mind your head, Em'leen, or the branches'll be hittin' you in the face."

They had left the cocoa-nut grove, and entered the chapparel. Here was a deeper twilight, and all sorts of trees lent their foliage to make the shade. The artu with its delicately diamonded trunk, the great breadfruit tall as a beech, and shadowy as a cave, the aoa, and the eternal cocoa-nut palm all grew here like brothers. Great ropes of wild vine twined like the snake of the laocoon from tree to tree, and all sorts of wonderful flowers, from the orchid shaped like a butterfly to the scarlet hibiscus, made beautiful the gloom.

Suddenly Mr. Button stopped.

"Whisht!" said he.

Through the silence—a silence filled with the hum and the murmur of wood insects and the faint, far song of the reef—came a tinkling, rippling sound: it was water. He listened to make sure of the bearing of the sound, then he made for it.

Next moment they found themselves in a little grass-grown glade. From the hilly ground above, over a rock black and polished like ebony, fell a tiny cascade not much broader than one's hand; ferns grew around and from a tree above where a great rope of wild convolvulus flowers blew their trumpets in the enchanted twilight.

The children cried out at the prettiness of it, and Emmeline ran and dabbled her hands in the water. Just above the little waterfall sprang a banana tree laden with fruit; it had immense leaves six feet long and more, and broad as a dinner-table. One could see the golden glint of the ripe fruit through the foliage.

In a moment Mr. Button had kicked off his shoes and was going up the rock like a cat, absolutely, for it seemed to give him nothing to climb by.

"Hurroo!" cried Dick in admiration. "Look at Paddy!"

Emmeline looked, and saw nothing but swaying leaves.

"Stand from under!" he shouted, and next moment down came a huge bunch of yellow-jacketed bananas. Dick shouted with delight, but Emmeline showed no excitement: she had discovered something.

XIII

DEATH VEILED WITH LICHEN

Mr. Button," said she, when the latter had descended, "there's a little barrel"; she pointed to something green and lichen-covered that lay between the trunks of two trees—something that eyes less sharp than the eyes of a child might have mistaken for a boulder.

"Sure, an' faith it's an' ould empty bar'l," said Mr. Button, wiping the sweat from his brow and staring at the thing. "Some ship must have been wathering here an' forgot it. It'll do for a sate whilst we have dinner."

He sat down upon it and distributed the bananas to the children, who sat down on the grass.

The barrel looked such a deserted and neglected thing that his imagination assumed it to be empty. Empty or full, however, it made an excellent seat, for it was quarter sunk in the green soft earth, and immovable.

"If ships has been here, ships will come again," said he, as he munched his bananas.

"Will daddy's ship come here?" asked Dick.

"Ay, to be sure it will," replied the other, taking out his pipe. "Now run about and play with the flowers an' lave me alone to smoke a pipe, and then we'll all go to the top of the hill beyant, and have a look round us.

"Come 'long, Em!" cried Dick; and the children started off amongst the trees, Dick pulling at the hanging vine tendrils, and Emmeline plucking what blossoms she could find within her small reach.

When he had finished his pipe he hallooed, and small voices answered him from the wood. Then the children came running back, Emmeline laughing and showing her small white teeth, a large bunch of blossoms in her hand; Dick flowerless, but carrying what seemed a large green stone.

"Look at what a funny thing I've found!" he cried; "it's got holes in it."

"Dhrap it!" shouted Mr. Button, springing from the barrel as if someone had stuck an awl into him. "Where'd you find it? What d'you mane by touchin' it? Give it here."

He took it gingerly in his hands; it was a lichen-covered skull, with a great dent in the back of it where it had been cloven by an axe or some sharp instrument. He hove it as far as he could away amidst the trees.

"What is it, Paddy?" asked Dick, half astonished, half frightened at the old man's manner.

"It's nothin' good," replied Mr. Button.

"There were two others, and I wanted to fetch them," grumbled Dick.

"You lave them alone. Musha! musha! but there's been black doin's here in days gone by. What is it, Emmeline?"

Emmeline was holding out her bunch of flowers for admiration. He took a great gaudy blossom—if flowers can ever be called gaudy—and stuck its stalk in the pocket of his coat. Then he led the way uphill, muttering as he went.

The higher they got the less dense became the trees and the fewer the cocoa-nut palms. The cocoa-nut palm loves the sea, and the few they had here all had their heads bent in the direction of the lagoon, as if yearning after it.

They passed a cane-brake where canes twenty feet high whispered together like bulrushes. Then a sunlit sward, destitute of tree or shrub, led them sharply upward for a hundred feet or so to where a great rock, the highest point of the island, stood, casting its shadow in the sunshine. The rock was about twenty feet high, and easy to climb. Its top was almost flat, and as spacious as an ordinary dinner-table. From it one could obtain a complete view of the island and the sea.

Looking down, one's eye travelled over the trembling and waving tree-tops, to the lagoon; beyond the lagoon to the reef, beyond the reef to the infinite space of the Pacific. The reef encircled the whole island, here further from the land, here closer; the song of the surf on it came as a whisper, just like the whisper you hear in a shell; but, a strange thing, though the sound heard on the beach was continuous, up here one could distinguish an intermittency as breaker after breaker dashed itself to death on the coral strand below.

You have seen a field of green barley ruffled over by the wind, just so from the hill-top you could see the wind in its passage over the sunlit foliage beneath.

It was breezing up from the south-west, and banyan and cocoa-palm, artu and breadfruit tree, swayed and rocked in the merry wind. So bright and moving was the picture of the breeze-swept sea, the blue lagoon, the foam-dashed reef, and the rocking trees that one felt one had surprised some mysterious gala day, some festival of Nature more than ordinarily glad.

As if to strengthen the idea, now and then above the trees would burst what seemed a rocket of coloured stars. The stars would drift away in a flock on the wind and be lost. They were flights of birds. All-coloured birds peopled the trees below—blue, scarlet, dove-coloured, bright of eye, but voiceless. From the reef you could see occasionally the sea-gulls rising here and there in clouds like small puffs of smoke.

The lagoon, here deep, here shallow, presented, according to its depth or shallowness, the colours of ultra-marine or sky. The broadest parts were the palest, because the most shallow; and here and there, in the shallows, you might see a faint tracery of coral ribs almost reaching the surface. The island at its broadest might have been three miles across. There was not a sign of house or habitation to be seen, and not a sail on the whole of the wide Pacific.

It was a strange place to be, up here. To find oneself surrounded by grass and flowers and trees, and all the kindliness of nature, to feel the breeze blow, to smoke one's pipe, and to remember that one was in a place uninhabited and unknown. A place to which no messages were ever carried except by the wind or the sea-gulls.

In this solitude the beetle was as carefully painted and the flower as carefully tended as though all the peoples of the civilised world were standing by to criticise or approve.

Nowhere in the world, perhaps, so well as here, could you appreciate Nature's splendid indifference to the great affairs of Man.

The old sailor was thinking nothing of this sort. His eyes were fixed on a small and almost imperceptible stain on the horizon to the sou'-sou'-west. It was no doubt another island almost hull-down on the horizon. Save for this blemish the whole wheel of the sea was empty and serene.

Emmeline had not followed them up to the rock. She had gone botanising where some bushes displayed great bunches of the crimson arita berries as if to show to the sun what Earth could do in the way of manufacturing poison. She plucked two great bunches of them, and with this treasure came to the base of the rock.

"Lave thim berries down!" cried MrButton, when she had attracted his attention. "Don't put thim in your mouth; thim's the never-wake-up berries."

He came down off the rock, hand over fist, flung the poisonous things away, and looked into Emmeline's small mouth, which at his

HENRY DE VERE STACPOOLE

command she opened wide. There was only a little pink tongue in it, however, curled up like a rose-leaf; no sign of berries or poison. So, giving her a little shake, just as a nursemaid would have done in like circumstances, he took Dick off the rock, and led the way back to the beach.

XIV

Echoes of Fairy-Land

"M r. Button," said Emmeline that night, as they sat on the sand near the tent he had improvised, "Mr. Button—cats go to sleep." They had been questioning him about the "never-wake-up" berries.

"Who said they didn't?" asked Mr. Button.

"I mean," said Emmeline, "they go to sleep and never wake up again. Ours did. It had stripes on it, and a white chest, and rings all down its tail. It went asleep in the garden, all stretched out, and showing its teeth; an' I told Jane, and Dicky ran in an' told uncle. I went to Mrs. Sims, the doctor's wife, to tea; and when I came back I asked Jane where pussy was—and she said it was deadn' berried, but I wasn't to tell uncle."

"I remember," said Dick. "It was the day I went to the circus, and you told me not to tell daddy the cat was deadn' berried. But I told Mrs. James's man when he came to do the garden; and I asked him where cats went when they were deadn' berried, and he said he guessed they went to hell—at least he hoped they did, for they were always scratchin' up the flowers. Then he told me not to tell anyone he'd said that, for it was a swear word, and he oughtn't to have said it. I asked him what he'd give me if I didn't tell, an' he gave me five cents. That was the day I bought the cocoa-nut."

The tent, a makeshift affair, consisting of two sculls and a tree branch, which Mr. Button had sawed off from a dwarf aoa, and the stay-sail he had brought from the brig, was pitched in the centre of the beach, so as to be out of the way of falling cocoa-nuts, should the breeze strengthen during the night. The sun had set, but the moon had not yet risen as they sat in the starlight on the sand near the temporary abode.

"What's the things you said made the boots for the people, Paddy?" asked Dick, after a pause.

"Which things?"

"You said in the wood I wasn't to talk, else—"

"Oh, the Cluricaunes—the little men that cobbles the Good People's brogues. Is it them you mane?"

"Yes," said Dick, not knowing quite whether it was them or not that he meant, but anxious for information that he felt would be curious. "And what are the good people?"

"Sure, where were you born and bred that you don't know the Good People is the other name for the fairies—savin' their presence?"

"There aren't any," replied Dick. "Mrs. Sims said there weren't."

"Mrs. James," put in Emmeline, "said there were. She said she liked to see children b'lieve in fairies. She was talking to another lady, who'd got a red feather in her bonnet, and a fur muff. They were having tea, and I was sitting on the hearthrug. She said the world was getting too—something or another, an' then the other lady said it was, and asked Mrs. James did she see Mrs. Someone in the awful hat she wore Thanksgiving Day. They didn't say anything more about fairies, but Mrs. James—"

"Whether you b'lave in them or not," said Paddy, "there they are. An' maybe they're poppin' out of the wood behint us now, an' listenin' to us talkin'; though I'm doubtful if there's any in these parts, though down in Connaught they were as thick as blackberries in the ould days. O musha! musha! the ould days, the ould days! when will I be seein' thim again? Now, you may b'lave me or b'lave me not, but me own ould father— God rest his sowl!—was comin' over Croagh Patrick one night before Christmas with a bottle of whisky in one hand of him, and a goose, plucked an' claned an' all, in the other, which same he'd won in a lottery, when, hearin' a tchune no louder than the buzzin' of a bee, over a furze-bush he peeps, and there, round a big white stone, the Good People were dancing in a ring hand in hand, an' kickin' their heels, an' the eyes of them glowin' like the eyes of moths; and a chap on the stone, no bigger than the joint of your thumb, playin' to thim on a bagpipes. Wid that he let wan yell an' drops the goose an' makes for home, over hedge an' ditch, boundin' like a buck kangaroo, an' the face on him as white as flour when he burst in through the door, where we was all sittin' round the fire burnin' chestnuts to see who'd be married the first.

"'An' what in the name of the saints is the mather wid yiz?' says me mother.

"'I've sane the Good People,' says he, 'up on the field beyant,' says he; 'and they've got the goose,' says he, 'but, begorra, I've saved the bottle,' he says. 'Dhraw the cork and give me a taste of it, for me heart's in me throat, and me tongue's like a brick-kil.'

"An' whin we come to prize the cork out of the bottle, there was nothin' in it; an' whin we went next marnin' to look for the goose, it was gone. But there was the stone, sure enough, and the marks on it of the little brogues of the chap that'd played the bagpipes—and who'd be doubtin' there were fairies after that?"

The children said nothing for a while, and then Dick said:

"Tell us about Cluricaunes, and how they make the boots."

"Whin I'm tellin' you about Cluricaunes," said Mr. Button, "it's the truth I'm tellin' you, an' out of me own knowlidge, for I've spoken to a man that's held wan in his hand; he was me own mother's brother, Con Cogan—rest his sowl! Con was six fut two, wid a long, white face; he'd had his head bashed in, years before I was barn, in some ruction or other, an' the docthers had japanned him with a five-shillin' piece beat flat."

Dick interposed with a question as to the process, aim, and object of japanning, but Mr. Button passed the question by.

"He'd been bad enough for seein' fairies before they japanned him, but afther it, begorra, he was twiced as bad. I was a slip of a lad at the time, but me hair near turned grey wid the tales he'd tell of the Good People and their doin's. One night they'd turn him into a harse an' ride him half over the county, wan chap on his back an' another runnin' behind, shovin' furze prickles under his tail to make him bucklep. Another night it's a dunkey he'd be, harnessed to a little cart, an' bein' kicked in the belly and made to draw stones. Thin it's a goose he'd be, runnin' over the common wid his neck stritched out squawkin', an' an old fairy woman afther him wid a knife, till it fair drove him to the dhrink; though, by the same token, he didn't want much dhrivin'.

"And what does he do when his money was gone, but tear the five-shillin' piece they'd japanned him wid aff the top of his hed, and swaps it for a bottle of whisky, and that was the end of him."

Mr. Button paused to relight his pipe, which had gone out, and there was silence for a moment.

The moon had risen, and the song of the surf on the reef filled the whole night with its lullaby. The broad lagoon lay waving and rippling in the moonlight to the incoming tide. Twice as broad it always looked seen by moonlight or starlight than when seen by day. Occasionally the splash of a great fish would cross the silence, and the ripple of it would pass a moment later across the placid water.

Big things happened in the lagoon at night, unseen by eyes from the shore. You would have found the wood behind them, had you walked through it, full of light. A tropic forest under a tropic moon is green as a sea cave. You can see the vine tendrils and the flowers, the orchids and tree boles all lit as by the light of an emerald-tinted day.

Mr. Button took a long piece of string from his pocket.

"It's bedtime," said he; "and I'm going to tether Em'leen, for fear she'd be walkin' in her slape, and wandherin' away an' bein' lost in the woods."

"I don't want to be tethered," said Emmeline.

"It's for your own good I'm doin' it," replied Mr. Button, fixing the string round her waist. "Now come 'long."

He led her like a dog in a leash to the tent, and tied the other end of the string to the scull, which was the tent's main prop and support.

"Now," said he, "if you be gettin' up and walkin' about in the night, it's down the tint will be on top of us all."

And, sure enough, in the small hours of the morning, it was.

XV

Fair Pictures in the Blue

I don't want my old britches on! I don't want my old britches on!"
Dick was darting about naked on the sand, Mr. Button after him
with a pair of small trousers in his hand. A crab might just as well have
attempted to chase an antelope.

They had been on the island a fortnight, and Dick had discovered
the keenest joy in life—to be naked. To be naked and wallow in the
shallows of the lagoon, to be naked and sit drying in the sun. To be free
from the curse of clothes, to shed civilisation on the beach in the form
of breeches, boots, coat, and hat, and to be one with the wind and the
sun and the sea.

The very first command Mr. Button had given on the second
morning of their arrival was, "Strip and into the water wid you."

Dick had resisted at first, and Emmeline (who rarely wept) had
stood weeping in her little chemise. But Mr. Button was obdurate. The
difficulty at first was to get them in; the difficulty now was to keep
them out.

Emmeline was sitting as nude as the day star, drying in the morning
sun after her dip, and watching Dick's evolutions on the sand.

The lagoon had for the children far more attraction than the land.
Woods where you might knock ripe bananas off the trees with a big cane,
sands where golden lizards would scuttle about so tame that you might
with a little caution seize them by the tail, a hill-top from whence you
might see, to use Paddy's expression, "to the back of beyond"; all these
were fine enough in their way, but they were nothing to the lagoon.

Deep down where the coral branches were you might watch, whilst
Paddy fished, all sorts of things disporting on the sand patches and
between the coral tufts. Hermit crabs that had evicted whelks, wearing
the evicted ones' shells—an obvious misfit; sea anemones as big as roses.
Flowers that closed up in an irritable manner if you lowered the hook
gently down and touched them; extraordinary shells that walked about
on feelers, elbowing the crabs out of the way and terrorising the whelks.
The overlords of the sand patches, these; yet touch one on the back with
a stone tied to a bit of string, and down he would go flat, motionless

HENRY DE VERE STACPOOLE

and feigning death. There was a lot of human nature lurking in the depths of the lagoon, comedy and tragedy.

An English rock-pool has its marvels. You can fancy the marvels of this vast rock-pool, nine miles round and varying from a third to half a mile broad, swarming with tropic life and flights of painted fishes; where the glittering albicore passed beneath the boat like a fire and a shadow; where the boat's reflection lay as clear on the bottom as though the water were air; where the sea, pacified by the reef, told, like a little child, its dreams.

It suited the lazy humour of Mr. Button that he never pursued the lagoon more than half a mile or so on either side of the beach. He would bring the fish he caught ashore, and with the aid of his tinder box and dead sticks make a blazing fire on the sand; cook fish and breadfruit and taro roots, helped and hindered by the children. They fixed the tent amidst the trees at the edge of the chapparel, and made it larger and more abiding with the aid of the dinghy's sail.

Amidst these occupations, wonders, and pleasures, the children lost all count of the flight of time. They rarely asked about Mr. Lestrange; after a while they did not ask about him at all. Children soon forget.

PART III

XVI

The Poetry of Learning

To forget the passage of time you must live in the open air, in a warm climate, with as few clothes as possible upon you. You must collect and cook your own food. Then, after a while, if you have no special ties to bind you to civilisation, Nature will begin to do for you what she does for the savage. You will recognise that it is possible to be happy without books or newspapers, letters or bills. You will recognise the part sleep plays in Nature.

After a month on the island you might have seen Dick at one moment full of life and activity, helping Mr. Button to dig up a taro root or what not, the next curled up to sleep like a dog. Emmeline the same. Profound and prolonged lapses into sleep; sudden awakenings into a world of pure air and dazzling light, the gaiety of colour all round. Nature had indeed opened her doors to these children.

One might have fancied her in an experimental mood, saying: "Let me put these buds of civilisation back into my nursery and see what they will become—how they will blossom, and what will be the end of it all."

Just as Emmeline had brought away her treasured box from the *Northumberland*, Dick had conveyed with him a small linen bag that chinked when shaken. It contained marbles. Small olive-green marbles and middle-sized ones of various colours; glass marbles with splendid coloured cores; and one large old grandfather marble too big to be played with, but none the less to be worshipped—a god marble.

Of course one cannot play at marbles on board ship, but one can play *with* them. They had been a great comfort to Dick on the voyage. He knew them each personally, and he would roll them out on the mattress of his bunk and review them nearly everyday, whilst Emmeline looked on.

One day Mr. Button, noticing Dick and the girl kneeling opposite each other on a flat, hard piece of sand near the water's edge, strolled up to see what they were doing. They were playing marbles. He stood with his hands in his pockets and his pipe in his mouth watching and criticising the game, pleased that the "childer" were amused. Then he began to be amused himself, and in a few minutes more he was down on his knees taking a hand; Emmeline, a poor player and an unenthusiastic one, withdrawing in his favour.

After that it was a common thing to see them playing together, the old sailor on his knees, one eye shut, and a marble against the nail of his horny thumb taking aim; Dick and Emmeline on the watch to make sure he was playing fair, their shrill voices echoing amidst the cocoa-nut trees with cries of "Knuckle down, Paddy, knuckle down!" He entered into all their amusements just as one of themselves. On high and rare occasions Emmeline would open her precious box, spread its contents and give a tea-party, Mr. Button acting as guest or president as the case might be.

"Is your tay to your likin', ma'am?" he would enquire; and Emmeline, sipping at her tiny cup, would invariably make answer: "Another lump of sugar, if you please, Mr. Button"; to which would come the stereotyped reply: "Take a dozen, and welcome; and another cup for the good of your make."

Then Emmeline would wash the things in imaginary water, replace them in the box, and everyone would lose their company manners and become quite natural again.

"Have you ever seen your name, Paddy?" asked Dick one morning.

"Seen me which?"

"Your name?"

"Arrah, don't be axin' me questions," replied the other. "How the divil could I see me name?"

"Wait and I'll show you," replied Dick.

He ran and fetched a piece of cane, and a minute later on the salt-white sand in face of orthography and the sun appeared these portentous letters:

BUTTEN

"Faith, an' it's a cliver boy y'are," said Mr. Button admiringly, as he leaned luxuriously against a cocoa-nut tree, and contemplated Dick's handiwork. "And that's me name, is it? What's the letters in it?"

Dick enumerated them.

"I'll teach you to do it, too," he said. "I'll teach you to write your name, Paddy—would you like to write your name, Paddy?"

"No," replied the other, who only wanted to be let smoke his pipe in peace; "me name's no use to me."

But Dick, with the terrible gadfly tirelessness of childhood, was not to be put off, and the unfortunate Mr. Button had to go to school despite himself. In a few days he could achieve the act of drawing upon the sand characters somewhat like the above, but not without prompting, Dick and Emmeline on each side of him, breathless for fear of a mistake.

"Which next?" would ask the sweating scribe, the perspiration pouring from his forehead—"which next? an' be quick, for it's moithered I am."

"N. N.—that's right—Ow, you're making it crooked!—*that's* right—there! it's all there now—Hurroo!"

"Hurroo!" would answer the scholar, waving his old hat over his own name, and "Hurroo!" would answer the cocoa-nut grove echoes; whilst the far, faint "Hi hi!" of the wheeling gulls on the reef would come over the blue lagoon as if in acknowledgment of the deed, and encouragement.

The appetite comes with teaching. The pleasantest mental exercise of childhood is the instruction of one's elders. Even Emmeline felt this. She took the geography class one day in a timid manner, putting her little hand first in the great horny fist of her friend.

"Mr. Button!"

"Well, honey?"

"I know g'ography."

"And what's that?" asked Mr. Button.

This stumped Emmeline for a moment.

"It's where places are," she said at last.

"Which places?" enquired he.

"All sorts of places," replied Emmeline. "Mr. Button!"

"What is it, darlin'?"

"Would you like to learn g'ography?"

"I'm not wishful for larnin'," said the other hurriedly. "It makes me head buzz to hear them things they rade out of books."

"Paddy," said Dick, who was strong on drawing that afternoon, "look here." He drew the following on the sand:

"That's an elephant," he said in a dubious voice.

Mr. Button grunted, and the sound was by no means filled with enthusiastic assent. A chill fell on the proceedings.

Dick wiped the elephant slowly and regretfully out, whilst Emmeline felt disheartened. Then her face suddenly cleared; the seraphic smile came into it for a moment—a bright idea had struck her.

"Dicky," she said, "draw Henry the Eight."

Dick's face brightened. He cleared the sand and drew the following figure:

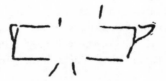

"*That's* not Henry the Eight," he explained, "but he will be in a minute. Daddy showed me how to draw him; he's nothing till he gets his hat on."

"Put his hat on, put his hat on!" implored Emmeline, gazing alternately from the figure on the sand to Mr. Button's face, watching for the delighted smile with which she was sure the old man would greet the great king when he appeared in all his glory.

Then Dick with a single stroke of the cane put Henry's hat on.

Now, no portrait could be liker to his monk-hunting majesty than the above, created with one stroke of a cane (so to speak), yet Mr. Button remained unmoved.

"I did it for Mrs. Sims," said Dick regretfully, "and *she* said it was the image of him."

"Maybe the hat's not big enough," said Emmeline, turning her head from side to side as she gazed at the picture. It looked right, but she felt there must be something wrong, as Mr. Button did not applaud. Has not every true artist felt the same before the silence of some critic?

Mr. Button tapped the ashes out of his pipe and rose to stretch himself, and the class rose and trooped down to the lagoon edge, leaving Henry and his hat a figure on the sand to be obliterated by the wind.

After a while, as time went on, Mr. Button took to his lessons as a matter of course, the small inventions of the children assisting their utterly untrustworthy knowledge. Knowledge, perhaps, as useful as any other there amidst the lovely poetry of the palm trees and the sky.

Days slipped into weeks, and weeks into months, without the appearance of a ship—a fact which gave Mr. Button very little trouble; and even less to his charges, who were far too busy and amused to bother about ships.

The rainy season came on them with a rush, and at the words "rainy season" do not conjure up in your mind the vision of a rainy day in Manchester.

The rainy season here was quite a lively time. Torrential showers followed by bursts of sunshine, rainbows, and rain-dogs in the sky, and the delicious perfume of all manner of growing things on the earth.

After the rains the old sailor said he'd be after making a house of bamboos before the next rains came on them; but, maybe, before that they'd be off the island.

"However," said he, "I'll dra' you a picture of what it'll be like when it's up"; and on the sand he drew a figure like this:

Having thus drawn the plans of the building, he leaned back against a cocoa-palm and lit his pipe. But he had reckoned without Dick.

The boy had not the least wish to live in a house, but he had a keen desire to see one built, and help to build one. The ingenuity which is part of the multiform basis of the American nature was aroused.

"How're you going to keep them from slipping, if you tie them together like that?" he asked, when Paddy had more fully explained his method.

"Which from slippin'?"

"The canes—one from the other?"

"After you've fixed thim, one cross t'other, you drive a nail through the cross-piece and a rope over all."

"Have you any nails, Paddy?"

"No," said Mr. Button, "I haven't."

"Then how're you goin' to build the house?"

"Ax me no questions now; I want to smoke me pipe."

But he had raised a devil difficult to lay. Morning, noon, and night it was "Paddy, when are you going to begin the house?" or, "Paddy, I guess I've got a way to make the canes stick together without nailing." Till Mr. Button, in despair, like a beaver, began to build.

There was great cane-cutting in the cane-brake above, and, when sufficient had been procured, Mr. Button struck work for three days. He would have struck altogether, but he had found a taskmaster.

The tireless Dick, young and active, with no original laziness in his composition, no old bones to rest, or pipe to smoke, kept after him like a bluebottle fly. It was in vain that he tried to stave him off with stories about fairies and Cluricaunes. Dick wanted to build a house.

Mr. Button didn't. He wanted to rest. He did not mind fishing or climbing a cocoa-nut tree, which he did to admiration by passing a rope round himself and the tree, knotting it, and using it as a support during the climb; but house-building was monotonous work.

He said he had no nails. Dick countered by showing how the canes could be held together by notching them.

"And, faith, but it's a cliver boy you are," said the weary one admiringly, when the other had explained his method.

"Then come along, Paddy, and stick 'em up."

Mr. Button said he had no rope, that he'd have to think about it, that tomorrow or next day he'd be after getting some notion how to do it without rope. But Dick pointed out that the brown cloth which Nature has wrapped round the cocoa-palm stalks would do instead of rope if cut in strips. Then the badgered one gave in.

They laboured for a fortnight at the thing, and at the end of that time had produced a rough sort of wigwam on the borders of the chapparel.

Out on the reef, to which they often rowed in the dinghy, when the tide was low, deep pools would be left, and in the pools fish. Paddy said if they had a spear they might be able to spear some of these fish, as he had seen the natives do away "beyant" in Tahiti.

Dick enquired as to the nature of a spear, and next day produced a ten-foot cane sharpened at the end after the fashion of a quill pen.

"Sure, what's the use of that?" said Mr. Button. "You might job it into a fish, but he'd be aff it in two ticks; it's the barb that holds them."

Next day the indefatigable one produced the cane amended; he had whittled it down about three feet from the end and on one side, and carved a fairly efficient barb. It was good enough, at all events, to spear a "groper" with, that evening, in the sunset-lit pools of the reef at low tide.

"There aren't any potatoes here," said Dick one day, after the second rains.

"We've et 'em all months ago," replied Paddy.

"How do potatoes grow?" enquired Dick.

"Grow, is it? Why, they grow in the ground; and where else would they grow?" He explained the process of potato-planting: cutting them into pieces so that there was an eye in each piece, and so forth. "Having done this," said Mr. Button, "you just chuck the pieces in the ground; their eyes grow, green leaves 'pop up,' and then, if you dug the roots up maybe, six months after, you'd find bushels of potatoes in the ground, ones as big as your head, and weeny ones. It's like a family of childer— some's big and some's little. But there they are in the ground, and all you have to do is to take a fark and dig a potful of them with a turn of your wrist, as many a time I've done it in the ould days."

"Why didn't we do that?" asked Dick.

"Do what?" asked Mr. Button.

"Plant some of the potatoes."

"And where'd we have found the spade to plant them with?"

"I guess we could have fixed up a spade," replied the boy. "I made a spade at home, out of a piece of old board, once—daddy helped."

"Well, skelp off with you, and make a spade now," replied the other, who wanted to be quiet and think, "and you and Em'line can dig in the sand."

Emmeline was sitting near by, stringing together some gorgeous blossoms on a tendril of liana. Months of sun and ozone had made a considerable difference in the child. She was as brown as a gipsy and freckled, not very much taller, but twice as plump. Her eyes had lost considerably that look as though she were contemplating futurity and immensity—not as abstractions, but as concrete images, and she had lost the habit of sleep-walking.

The shock of the tent coming down on the first night she was tethered to the scull had broken her of it, helped by the new healthful conditions of life, the sea-bathing, and the eternal open air. There is no narcotic to excel fresh air.

Months of semi-savagery had made also a good deal of difference in Dick's appearance. He was two inches taller than on the day they landed. Freckled and tanned, he had the appearance of a boy of twelve. He was the promise of a fine man. He was not a good-looking child, but he was healthy-looking, with a jolly laugh, and a daring, almost impudent expression of face.

The question of the children's clothes was beginning to vex the mind of the old sailor. The climate was a suit of clothes in itself. One was much happier with almost nothing on. Of course there were changes of temperature, but they were slight. Eternal summer, broken by torrential rains, and occasionally a storm, that was the climate of the island; still, the "childer" couldn't go about with nothing on.

He took some of the striped flannel and made Emmeline a kilt. It was funny to see him sitting on the sand, Emmeline standing before him with her garment round her waist, being tried on; he, with a mouthful of pins, and the housewife with the scissors, needles, and thread by his side.

"Turn to the lift a bit more," he'd say, "aisy does it. Stidy so—musha! musha! where's thim scissors? Dick, be holdin' the end of this bit of string till I get the stitches in behint. Does that hang comfortable?— well, an' you're the trouble an' all. How's *that*? That's aisier, is it? Lift your fut till I see if it comes to your knees. Now off with it, and lave me alone till I stitch the tags to it."

It was the mixture of a skirt and the idea of a sail, for it had two rows of reef points; a most ingenious idea, as it could be reefed if the child wanted to go paddling, or in windy weather.

XVII

THE DEVIL'S CASK

One morning, about a week after the day on which the old sailor, to use his own expression, had bent a skirt on Emmeline, Dick came through the woods and across the sands running. He had been on the hill-top.

"Paddy," he cried to the old man, who was fixing a hook on a fishing-line, "there's a ship!"

It did not take Mr. Button long to reach the hill-top, and there she was, beating up for the island. Bluff-bowed and squab, the figure of an old Dutch woman, and telling of her trade a league off. It was just after the rains, the sky was not yet quite clear of clouds; you could see showers away at sea, and the sea was green and foam-capped.

There was the trying-out gear; there were the boats, the crow's nest, and all complete, and labelling her a whaler. She was a ship, no doubt, but Paddy Button would as soon have gone on board a ship manned by devils, and captained by Lucifer, as on board a South Sea whaleman. He had been there before, and he knew.

He hid the children under a large banyan, and told them not to stir or breathe till he came back, for the ship was "the devil's own ship"; and if the men on board caught them they'd skin them alive and all.

Then he made for the beach; he collected all the things out of the wigwam, and all the old truck in the shape of boots and old clothes, and stowed them away in the dinghy. He would have destroyed the house, if he could, but he hadn't time. Then he rowed the dinghy a hundred yards down the lagoon to the left, and moored her under the shade of an aoa, whose branches grew right over the water. Then he came back through the cocoa-nut grove on foot, and peered through the trees over the lagoon to see what was to be seen.

The wind was blowing dead on for the opening in the reef, and the old whaleman came along breasting the swell with her bluff bows, and entered the lagoon. There was no leadsman in her chains. She just came in as if she knew all the soundings by heart—as probably she did—for these whalemen know every hole and corner in the Pacific.

The anchor fell with a splash, and she swung to it, making a strange enough picture as she floated on the blue mirror, backed by the graceful palm tree on the reef. Then Mr. Button, without waiting to see the boats lowered, made back to his charges, and the three camped in the woods that night.

Next morning the whaleman was off and away, leaving as a token of her visit the white sand all trampled, an empty bottle, half an old newspaper, and the wigwam torn to pieces.

The old sailor cursed her and her crew, for the incident had brought a new exercise into his lazy life. Everyday now at noon he had to climb the hill, on the look-out for whalemen. Whalemen haunted his dreams, though I doubt if he would willingly have gone on board even a Royal Mail steamer. He was quite happy where he was. After long years of the fo'cs'le the island was a change indeed. He had tobacco enough to last him for an indefinite time, the children for companions, and food at his elbow. He would have been entirely happy if the island had only been supplied by Nature with a public-house.

The spirit of hilarity and good fellowship, however, who suddenly discovered this error on the part of Nature, rectified it, as will be presently seen.

The most disastrous result of the whaleman's visit was not the destruction of the "house," but the disappearance of Emmeline's box. Hunt high or hunt low, it could not be found. Mr. Button in his hurry must have forgotten it when he removed the things to the dinghy—at all events, it was gone. Probably one of the crew of the whalemen had found it and carried it off with him; no one could say. It was gone, and there was the end of the matter, and the beginning of great tribulation, that lasted Emmeline for a week.

She was intensely fond of coloured things, coloured flowers especially; and she had the prettiest way of making them into a wreath for her own or someone else's head. It was the hat-making instinct that was at work in her, perhaps; at all events, it was a feminine instinct, for Dick made no wreaths.

One morning, as she was sitting by the old sailor engaged in stringing shells, Dick came running along the edge of the grove. He had just come out of the wood, and he seemed to be looking for something. Then he found what he was in search of—a big shell—and with it in his hand made back to the wood.

Item.—His dress was a piece of cocoa-nut cloth tied round his middle. Why he wore it at all, goodness knows, for he would as often as not be running about stark naked.

"I've found something, Paddy!" he cried, as he disappeared among the trees.

"What have you found?" piped Emmeline, who was always interested in new things.

"Something funny!" came back from amidst the trees.

Presently he returned; but he was not running now. He was walking slowly and carefully, holding the shell as if it contained something precious that he was afraid would escape.

"Paddy, I turned over the old barrel and it had a cork thing in it, and I pulled it out, and the barrel is full of awfully funny-smelling stuff—I've brought some for you to see."

He gave the shell into the old sailor's hands. There was about half a gill of yellow liquid in the shell. Paddy smelt it, tasted, and gave a shout.

"Rum, begorra!"

"What is it, Paddy?" asked Emmeline.

"*Where* did you say you got it—in the ould bar'l, did you say?" asked Mr. Button, who seemed dazed and stunned as if by a blow.

"Yes; I pulled the cork thing out—"

"*Did yiz put it back?*"

"Yes."

"Oh, glory be to God! Here have I been, time out of mind, sittin' on an ould empty bar'l, with me tongue hangin' down to me heels for the want of a drink, and it full of rum all the while!"

He took a sip of the stuff, tossed the lot off, closed his lips tight to keep in the fumes, and shut one eye.

Emmeline laughed.

Mr. Button scrambled to his feet. They followed him through the chapparel till they reached the water source. There lay the little green barrel; turned over by the restless Dick, it lay with its bung pointing to the leaves above. You could see the hollow it had made in the soft soil during the years. So green was it, and so like an object of nature, a bit of old tree-bole, or a lichen-stained boulder, that though the whalemen had actually watered from the source, its real nature had not been discovered.

Mr. Button tapped on it with the butt end of the shell: it was nearly full. Why it had been left there, by whom, or how, there was no one to tell. The old lichen-covered skulls might have told, could they have spoken.

"We'll rowl it down to the beach," said Paddy, when he had taken another taste of it.

He gave Dick a sip. The boy spat it out, and made a face, then, pushing the barrel before them, they began to roll it downhill to the beach, Emmeline running before them crowned with flowers.

XVIII

The Rat Hunt

They had dinner at noon. Paddy knew how to cook fish, island fashion, wrapping them in leaves, and baking them in a hole in the ground in which a fire had previously been lit. They had fish and taro root baked, and green cocoa-nuts; and after dinner Mr. Button filled a big shell with rum, and lit his pipe.

The rum had been good originally, and age had improved it. Used as he was to the appalling balloon juice sold in the drinking dens of the "Barbary coast" at San Francisco, or the public-houses of the docks, this stuff was nectar.

Joviality radiated from him: it was infectious. The children felt that some happy influence had fallen upon their friend. Usually after dinner he was drowsy and "wishful to be quiet." Today he told them stories of the sea, and sang them songs—chantys:

> *"I'm a flyin' fish sailor come back from Hong Kong,*
> *Yeo ho! blow the man down.*
> *Blow the man down, bullies, blow the man down,*
> *Oh, give us* time *to blow the man down.*
> *You're a dhirty black-baller come back from New York,*
> *Yeo ho! blow the man down,*
> *Blow the man down, bullies, blow the man down.*
> *Oh, give us time to blow the man down."*

"Oh, give us *time* to blow the man down!" echoed Dick and Emmeline.

Up above, in the trees, the bright-eyed birds were watching them—such a happy party. They had all the appearance of picnickers, and the song echoed amongst the cocoa-nut trees, and the wind carried it over the lagoon to where the sea-gulls were wheeling and screaming, and the foam was thundering on the reef.

That evening, Mr. Button feeling inclined for joviality, and not wishing the children to see him under the influence, rolled the barrel through the cocoa-nut grove to a little clearing by the edge of the water. There, when the children were in bed and asleep, he repaired with some green cocoa-nuts and a shell. He was generally musical when amusing himself in this fashion, and Emmeline, waking up during the night, heard his voice borne through the moonlit cocoa-nut grove by the wind:

"There were five or six old drunken sailors
Standin' before the bar,
And Larry, he was servin' them
From a big five-gallon jar.

"Chorus.—
Hoist up the flag, long may it wave!
Long may it lade us to glory or the grave.
Stidy, boys, stidy—sound the jubilee,
For Babylon has fallen, and the niggers are all set free."

Next morning the musician awoke beside the cask. He had not a trace of a headache, or any bad feeling, but he made Dick do the cooking; and he lay in the shade of the cocoa-nut trees, with his head on a "pilla" made out of an old coat rolled up, twiddling his thumbs, smoking his pipe, and discoursing about the "ould" days, half to himself and half to his companions.

That night he had another musical evening all to himself, and so it went on for a week. Then he began to lose his appetite and sleep; and one morning Dick found him sitting on the sand looking very queer indeed—as well he might, for he had been "seeing things" since dawn.

"What is it, Paddy?" said the boy, running up, followed by Emmeline.

Mr. Button was staring at a point on the sand close by. He had his right hand raised after the manner of a person who is trying to catch a fly. Suddenly he made a grab at the sand, and then opened his hand wide to see what he had caught.

"What is it, Paddy?"

"The Cluricaune," replied Mr. Button. "All dressed in green he was—musha! musha! but it's only pretindin' I am."

The complaint from which he was suffering has this strange thing about it, that, though the patient sees rats, or snakes, or what not, as real-looking as the real things, and though they possess his mind for a moment, almost immediately he recognises that he is suffering from a delusion.

The children laughed, and Mr. Button laughed in a stupid sort of way.

HENRY DE VERE STACPOOLE

"Sure, it was only a game I was playin'—there was no Cluricaune at all—it's whin I dhrink rum it puts it into me head to play games like that. Oh, be the Holy Poker, there's red rats comin' out of the sand!"

He got on his hands and knees and scuttled off towards the cocoa-nut trees, looking over his shoulder with a bewildered expression on his face. He would have risen to fly, only he dared not stand up.

The children laughed and danced round him as he crawled.

"Look at the rats, Paddy! look at the rats!" cried Dick.

"They're in front of me!" cried the afflicted one, making a vicious grab at an imaginary rodent's tail. "Ran dan the bastes!—now they're gone. Musha, but it's a fool I'm makin' of meself."

"Go on, Paddy," said Dick; "don't stop—Look there—there's more rats coming after you!"

"Oh, whisht, will you?" replied Paddy, taking his seat on the sand, and wiping his brow. "They're aff me now."

The children stood by, disappointed of their game. Good acting appeals to children just as much as to grown-up people. They stood waiting for another access of humour to take the comedian, and they had not to wait long.

A thing like a flayed horse came out of the lagoon and up the beach, and this time Mr. Button did not crawl away. He got on his feet and ran.

"It's a harse that's afther me—it's a harse that's afther me! Dick! Dick! hit him a skelp. Dick! Dick! dhrive him away."

"Hurroo! Hurroo!" cried Dick, chasing the afflicted one, who was running in a wide circle, his broad red face slewed over his left shoulder. "Go it, Paddy! go it, Paddy!"

"Kape off me, you baste!" shouted Paddy. "Holy Mary, Mother of God! I'll land you a kick wid me fut if yiz come nigh me. Em'leen! Em'leen! come betune us!"

He tripped, and over he went on the sand, the indefatigable Dick beating him with a little switch he had picked up to make him continue.

"I'm better now, but I'm near wore out," said Mr. Button, sitting up on the sand. "But, bedad, if I'm chased by anymore things like them it's into the say I'll be dashin'. Dick, lend me your arum."

He took Dick's arm and wandered over to the shade of the trees. Here he threw himself down, and told the children to leave him to sleep. They recognised that the game was over and left him. And he slept for six hours on end; it was the first real sleep he had had for several days. When he awoke he was well, but very shaky.

XIX

STARLIGHT ON THE FOAM

Mr. Button saw no more rats, much to Dick's disappointment. He was off the drink. At dawn next day he got up, refreshed by a second sleep, and wandered down to the edge of the lagoon. The opening in the reef faced the east, and the light of the dawn came rippling in with the flooding tide.

"It's a baste I've been," said the repentant one—"a brute baste."

He was quite wrong; as a matter of fact, he was only a man beset and betrayed.

He stood for a while, cursing the drink, "and them that sells it." Then he determined to put himself out of the way of temptation. Pull the bung out of the barrel, and let the contents escape?

Such a thought never even occurred to him—or, if it did, was instantly dismissed; for, though an old sailor-man may curse the drink, good rum is to him a sacred thing; and to empty half a little barrel of it into the sea, would be an act almost equivalent to child-murder. He put the cask into the dinghy, and rowed it over to the reef. There he placed it in the shelter of a great lump of coral, and rowed back.

Paddy had been trained all his life to rhythmical drunkenness. Four months or so had generally elapsed between his bouts—sometimes six; it all depended on the length of the voyage. Six months now elapsed before he felt even an inclination to look at the rum cask, that tiny dark spot away on the reef. And it was just as well, for during those six months another whale-ship arrived, watered and was avoided.

"Blisther it!" said he; "the say here seems to breed whale-ships, and nothin' but whale-ships. It's like bugs in a bed: you kill wan, and then another comes. Howsomever, we're shut of thim for a while."

He walked down to the lagoon edge, looked at the little dark spot and whistled. Then he walked back to prepare dinner. That little dark spot began to trouble him after a while; not it, but the spirit it contained.

Days grew long and weary, the days that had been so short and pleasant. To the children there was no such thing as time. Having absolute and perfect health, they enjoyed happiness as far as mortals can enjoy it. Emmeline's highly-strung nervous system, it is true, developed

HENRY DE VERE STACPOOLE

a headache when she had been too long in the glare of the sun, but they were few and far between.

The spirit in the little cask had been whispering across the lagoon for some weeks; at last it began to shout. Mr. Button, metaphorically speaking, stopped his ears. He busied himself with the children as much as possible. He made another garment for Emmeline, and cut Dick's hair with the scissors (a job which was generally performed once in a couple of months).

One night, to keep the rum from troubling his head, he told them the story of Jack Dogherty and the Merrow, which is well known on the western coast.

The Merrow takes Jack to dinner at the bottom of the sea, and shows him the lobster pots wherein he keeps the souls of old sailor-men, and then they have dinner, and the Merrow produces a big bottle of rum.

It was a fatal story for him to remember and recount; for, after his companions were asleep, the vision of the Merrow and Jack hobnobbing, and the idea of the jollity of it, rose before him, and excited a thirst for joviality not to be resisted.

There were some green cocoa-nuts that he had plucked that day lying in a little heap under a tree—half a dozen or so. He took several of these and a shell, found the dinghy where it was moored to the aoa tree, unmoored her, and pushed off into the lagoon.

The lagoon and sky were full of stars. In the dark depths of the water might have been seen phosphorescent gleams of passing fish, and the thunder of the surf on the reef filled the night with its song.

He fixed the boat's painter carefully round a spike of coral and landed on the reef, and with a shellful of rum and cocoa-nut lemonade mixed half and half, he took his perch on a high ledge of coral from whence a view of the sea and the coral strand could be obtained.

On a moonlight night it was fine to sit here and watch the great breakers coming in, all marbled and clouded and rainbowed with spindrift and sheets of spray. But the snow and the song of them under the diffused light of the stars produced a more indescribably beautiful and strange effect.

The tide was going out now, and Mr. Button, as he sat smoking his pipe and drinking his grog, could see bright mirrors here and there where the water lay in rock-pools. When he had contemplated these sights for a considerable time in complete contentment, he returned to the lagoon side of the reef and sat down beside the little barrel. Then, after a while, if you had been standing on the strand opposite, you would have heard scraps of song borne across the quivering water of the lagoon.

> *"Sailing down, sailing down*
> *On the coast of Barbaree."*

Whether the coast of Barbary in question is that at San Francisco, or the true and proper coast, does not matter. It is an old-time song; and when you hear it, whether on a reef of coral or a granite quay, you may feel assured that an old-time sailor-man is singing it, and that the old-time sailor-man is bemused.

Presently the dinghy put off from the reef, the sculls broke the starlit waters and great shaking circles of light made rhythmical answer to the slow and steady creak of the thole pins against the leather. He tied up to the aoa, saw that the sculls were safely shipped; then, breathing heavily, he cast off his boots for fear of waking the "childer." As the children were sleeping more than two hundred yards away, this was a needless precaution—especially as the intervening distance was mostly soft sand.

Green cocoa-nut juice and rum mixed together are pleasant enough to drink, but they are better drunk separately; combined, not even the brain of an old sailor can make anything of them but mist and muddlement; that is to say, in the way of thought—in the way of action they can make him do a lot. They made Paddy Button swim the lagoon.

The recollection came to him all at once, as he was walking up the strand towards the wigwam, that he had left the dinghy tied to the reef. The dinghy was, as a matter of fact, safe and sound tied to the aoa; but Mr. Button's memory told him it was tied to the reef. How he had crossed the lagoon was of no importance at all to him; the fact that he had crossed without the boat, yet without getting wet, did not appear to him strange. He had no time to deal with trifles like these. The dinghy had to be fetched across the lagoon, and there was only one way of fetching it. So he came back down the beach to the water's edge, cast down his boots, cast off his coat, and plunged in. The lagoon was wide, but in his present state of mind he would have swum the Hellespont. His figure gone from the beach, the night resumed its majesty and aspect of meditation.

So lit was the lagoon by starshine that the head of the swimmer could be distinguished away out in the midst of circles of light; also, as the head neared the reef, a dark triangle that came shearing through the water past the palm tree at the pier. It was the night patrol of the lagoon, who had heard in some mysterious manner that a drunken sailor-man was making trouble in his waters.

Looking, one listened, hand on heart, for the scream of the arrested one, yet it did not come. The swimmer, scrambling on to the reef in an exhausted manner, forgetful evidently of the object for which he had returned, made for the rum cask, and fell down beside it as though sleep had touched him instead of death.

XX

The Dreamer on the Reef

I wonder where Paddy is?" cried Dick next morning. He was coming out of the chapparel pulling a dead branch after him. "He's left his coat on the sand, and the tinder box in it, so I'll make the fire. There's no use waiting. I want my breakfast. Bother—"

He trod the dead stick with his naked feet, breaking it into pieces.

Emmeline sat on the sand and watched him.

Emmeline had two gods of a sort: Paddy Button and Dick. Paddy was almost an esoteric god wrapped in the fumes of tobacco and mystery. The god of rolling ships and creaking masts—the masts and vast sail spaces of the *Northumberland* were an enduring vision in her mind— the deity who had lifted her from a little boat into this marvellous place, where the birds were coloured and the fish were painted, where life was never dull, and the skies scarcely ever grey.

Dick, the other deity, was a much more understandable personage, but no less admirable, as a companion and protector. In the two years and five months of island life he had grown nearly three inches. He was as strong as a boy of twelve, and could scull the boat almost as well as Paddy himself, and light a fire. Indeed, during the last few months Mr. Button, engaged in resting his bones, and contemplating rum as an abstract idea, had left the cooking and fishing and general gathering of food as much as possible to Dick.

"It amuses the craythur to pritind he's doing things," he would say, as he watched Dick delving in the earth to make a little oven— island-fashion—for the cooking of fish or what not.

"Come along, Em," said Dick, piling the broken wood on top of some rotten hibiscus sticks; "give me the tinder box."

He got a spark on to a bit of punk, and then he blew at it, looking not unlike Æolus as represented on those old Dutch charts that smell of schiedam and snuff, and give one mermaids and angels instead of soundings.

The fire was soon sparkling and crackling, and he heaped on sticks in profusion, for there was plenty of fuel, and he wanted to cook breadfruit.

The breadfruit varies in size, according to age, and in colour according to season. These that Dick was preparing to cook were as large as small melons. Two would be more than enough for three people's breakfast. They were green and knobbly on the outside, and they suggested to the mind unripe lemons, rather than bread.

He put them in the embers, just as you put potatoes to roast, and presently they sizzled and spat little venomous jets of steam, then they cracked, and the white inner substance became visible. He cut them open and took the core out—the core is not fit to eat—and they were ready.

Meanwhile, Emmeline, under his directions, had not been idle.

There were in the lagoon—there are in several other tropical lagoons I know of—a fish which I can only describe as a golden herring. A bronze herring it looks when landed, but when swimming away down against the background of coral brains and white sand patches, it has the sheen of burnished gold. It is as good to eat as to look at, and Emmeline was carefully toasting several of them on a piece of cane.

The juice of the fish kept the cane from charring, though there were accidents at times, when a whole fish would go into the fire, amidst shouts of derision from Dick.

She made a pretty enough picture as she knelt, the "skirt" round the waist looking not unlike a striped bath-towel, her small face intent, and filled with the seriousness of the job on hand, and her lips puckered out at the heat of the fire.

"It's so hot!" she cried in self-defence, after the first of the accidents.

"Of course it's hot," said Dick, "if you stick to looward of the fire. How often has Paddy told you to keep to windward of it!"

"I don't know which is which," confessed the unfortunate Emmeline, who was an absolute failure at everything practical: who could neither row nor fish, nor throw a stone, and who, though they had now been on the island twenty-eight months or so, could not even swim.

"You mean to say," said Dick, "that you don't know where the wind comes from?"

"Yes, I know that."

"Well, that's to windward."

"I didn't know that."

"Well, you know it now."

"Yes, I know it now."

"Well, then, come to windward of the fire. Why didn't you ask the meaning of it before?"

"I did," said Emmeline; "I asked Mr. Button one day, and he told me a lot about it. He said if he was to spit to windward and a person was to stand to loo'ard of him, he'd be a fool; and he said if a ship went too much to loo'ard she went on the rocks, but I didn't understand what he meant. Dicky, I wonder where he is?"

"Paddy!" cried Dick, pausing in the act of splitting open a breadfruit. Echoes came from amidst the cocoa-nut trees, but nothing more.

"Come on," said Dick; "I'm not going to wait for him. He may have gone to fetch up the night lines"—they sometimes put down night lines in the lagoon—"and fallen asleep over them."

Now, though Emmeline honoured Mr. Button as a minor deity, Dick had no illusions at all upon the matter. He admired Paddy because he could knot, and splice, and climb a cocoa-nut tree, and exercise his sailor craft in other admirable ways, but he felt the old man's limitations. They ought to have had potatoes now, but they had eaten both potatoes and the possibility of potatoes when they consumed the contents of that half sack. Young as he was, Dick felt the absolute thriftlessness of this proceeding. Emmeline did not; she never thought of potatoes, though she could have told you the colour of all the birds on the island.

Then, again, the house wanted rebuilding, and Mr. Button said everyday he would set about seeing after it tomorrow, and on the morrow it would be tomorrow. The necessities of the life they led were a stimulus to the daring and active mind of the boy; but he was always being checked by the go-as-you-please methods of his elder. Dick came of the people who make sewing machines and typewriters. Mr. Button came of a people notable for ballads, tender hearts, and potheen. That was the main difference.

"Paddy!" again cried the boy, when he had eaten as much as he wanted. "Hullo! where are you?"

They listened, but no answer came. A bright-hued bird flew across the sand space, a lizard scuttled across the glistening sand, the reef spoke, and the wind in the tree-tops; but Mr. Button made no reply.

"Wait," said Dick.

He ran through the grove towards the aoa where the dinghy was moored; then he returned.

"The dinghy is all right," he said. "Where on earth can he be?"

"I don't know," said Emmeline, upon whose heart a feeling of loneliness had fallen.

"Let's go up the hill," said Dick; "perhaps we'll find him there."

They went uphill through the wood, past the water-course. Every now and then Dick would call out, and echoes would answer—there were quaint, moist-voiced echoes amidst the trees—or a bevy of birds would take flight. The little waterfall gurgled and whispered, and the great banana leaves spread their shade.

"Come on," said Dick, when he had called again without receiving a reply.

They found the hill-top, and the great boulder stood casting its shadow in the sun. The morning breeze was blowing, the sea sparkling, the reef flashing, the foliage of the island waving in the wind like the flames of a green-flamed torch. A deep swell was spreading itself across the bosom of the Pacific. Some hurricane away beyond the Navigators or Gilberts had sent this message and was finding its echo here, a thousand miles away, in the deeper thunder of the reef.

Nowhere else in the world could you get such a picture, such a combination of splendour and summer, such a vision of freshness and strength, and the delight of morning. It was the smallness of the island, perhaps, that closed the charm and made it perfect. Just a bunch of foliage and flowers set in the midst of the blowing wind and sparkling blue.

Suddenly Dick, standing beside Emmeline on the rock, pointed with his finger to the reef near the opening.

"There he is!" cried he.

XXI

The Garland of Flowers

You could just make the figure out lying on the reef near the little cask, and comfortably sheltered from the sun by an upstanding lump of coral.

"He's asleep," said Dick.

He had not thought to look towards the reef from the beach, or he might have seen the figure before.

"Dicky!" said Emmeline.

"Well?"

"How did he get over, if you said the dinghy was tied to the tree?"

"I don't know," said Dick, who had not thought of this; "there he is, anyhow. I'll tell you what, Em, we'll row across and wake him. I'll boo into his ear and make him jump."

They got down from the rock, and came back down through the wood. As they came Emmeline picked flowers and began making them up into one of her wreaths. Some scarlet hibiscus, some bluebells, a couple of pale poppies with furry stalks and bitter perfume.

"What are you making that for?" asked Dick, who always viewed Emmeline's wreath-making with a mixture of compassion and vague disgust.

"I'm going to put it on Mr. Button's head," said Emmeline; "so's when you say boo into his ear he'll jump up with it on."

Dick chuckled with pleasure at the idea of the practical joke, and almost admitted in his own mind for a moment, that after all there might be a use for such futilities as wreaths.

The dinghy was moored under the spreading shade of the aoa, the painter tied to one of the branches that projected over the water. These dwarf aoas branch in an extraordinary way close to the ground, throwing out limbs like rails. The tree had made a good protection for the little boat, protecting it from marauding hands and from the sun; besides the protection of the tree Paddy had now and then scuttled the boat in shallow water. It was a new boat to start with, and with precautions like these might be expected to last many years.

"Get in," said Dick, pulling on the painter so that the bow of the dinghy came close to the beach.

Emmeline got carefully in, and went aft. Then Dick got in, pushed off, and took to the sculls. Next moment they were out on the sparkling water.

Dick rowed cautiously, fearing to wake the sleeper. He fastened the painter to the coral spike that seemed set there by nature for the purpose. He scrambled on to the reef, and lying down on his stomach drew the boat's gunwale close up so that Emmeline might land. He had no boots on; the soles of his feet, from constant exposure, had become insensitive as leather.

Emmeline also was without boots. The soles of her feet, as is always the case with highly nervous people, were sensitive, and she walked delicately, avoiding the worst places, holding her wreath in her right hand.

It was full tide, and the thunder of the waves outside shook the reef. It was like being in a church when the deep bass of the organ is turned full on, shaking the ground and the air, the walls and the roof. Dashes of spray came over with the wind, and the melancholy "Hi, hi!" of the wheeling gulls came like the voices of ghostly sailor-men hauling at the halyards.

Paddy was lying on his right side steeped in profound oblivion. His face was buried in the crook of his right arm, and his brown tattooed left hand lay on his left thigh, palm upwards. He had no hat, and the breeze stirred his grizzled hair.

Dick and Emmeline stole up to him till they got right beside him. Then Emmeline, flashing out a laugh, flung the little wreath of flowers on the old man's head, and Dick, popping down on his knees, shouted into his ear. But the dreamer did not stir or move a finger.

"Paddy," cried Dick, "wake up! wake up!"

He pulled at the shoulder till the figure from its sideways posture fell over on its back. The eyes were wide open and staring. The mouth hung open, and from the mouth darted a little crab; it scuttled over the chin and dropped on the coral.

Emmeline screamed, and screamed, and would have fallen, but the boy caught her in his arms—one side of the face had been destroyed by the larvæ of the rocks.

He held her to him as he stared at the terrible figure lying upon its back, hands outspread. Then, wild with terror, he dragged her towards the little boat. She was struggling, and panting and gasping, like a person drowning in ice-cold water.

His one instinct was to escape, to fly—anywhere, no matter where. He dragged the girl to the coral edge, and pulled the boat up close. Had the reef suddenly become enveloped in flames he could not have exerted himself more to escape from it and save his companion. A moment later they were afloat, and he was pulling wildly for the shore.

He did not know what had happened, nor did he pause to think: he was fleeing from horror—nameless horror; whilst the child at his feet, with her head resting against the gunwale, stared up open-eyed and speechless at the great blue sky, as if at some terror visible there. The boat grounded on the white sand, and the wash of the incoming tide drove it up sideways.

Emmeline had fallen forward; she had lost consciousness.

XXII

ALONE

The idea of spiritual life must be innate in the heart of man, for all that terrible night, when the children lay huddled together in the little hut in the chapparel, the fear that filled them was that their old friend might suddenly darken the entrance and seek to lie down beside them.

They did not speak about him. Something had been done to him; something had happened. Something terrible had happened to the world they knew. But they dared not speak of it or question each other.

Dick had carried his companion to the hut when he left the boat, and hidden with her there; the evening had come on, and the night, and now in the darkness, without having tasted food all day, he was telling her not to be afraid, that he would take care of her. But not a word of the thing that had happened.

The thing, for them, had no precedent, and no vocabulary. They had come across death raw and real, uncooked by religion, undeodorised by the sayings of sages and poets.

They knew nothing of the philosophy that tells us that death is the common lot, and the natural sequence to birth, or the religion that teaches us that Death is the door to Life.

A dead old sailor-man lying like a festering carcass on a coral ledge, eyes staring and glazed and fixed, a wide-open mouth that once had spoken comforting words, and now spoke living crabs.

That was the vision before them. They did not philosophise about it; and though they were filled with terror, I do not think it was terror that held them from speaking about it, but a vague feeling that what they had beheld was obscene, unspeakable, and a thing to avoid.

Lestrange had brought them up in his own way. He had told them there was a good God who looked after the world; determined as far as he could to exclude demonology and sin and death from their knowledge, he had rested content with the bald statement that there was a good God who looked after the world, without explaining fully that the same God would torture them forever and ever, should they fail to believe in Him or keep His commandments.

This knowledge of the Almighty, therefore, was but a half knowledge, the vaguest abstraction. Had they been brought up, however, in the most strictly Calvinistic school, this knowledge of Him would have been no comfort now. Belief in God is no comfort to a frightened child. Teach him as many parrot-like prayers as you please, and in distress or the dark of what use are they to him? His cry is for his nurse, or his mother.

During that dreadful night these two children had no comfort to seek anywhere in the whole wide universe but in each other. She, in a sense of his protection, he, in a sense of being her protector. The manliness in him greater and more beautiful than physical strength, developed in those dark hours just as a plant under extraordinary circumstances is hurried into bloom.

Towards dawn Emmeline fell asleep. Dick stole out of the hut when he had assured himself from her regular breathing that she was asleep, and, pushing the tendrils and the branches of the mammee apples aside, found the beach. The dawn was just breaking, and the morning breeze was coming in from the sea.

When he had beached the dinghy the day before, the tide was just at the flood, and it had left her stranded. The tide was coming in now, and in a short time it would be far enough up to push her off.

Emmeline in the night had implored him to take her away. Take her away somewhere from there, and he had promised, without knowing in the least how he was to perform his promise. As he stood looking at the beach, so desolate and strangely different now from what it was the day before, an idea of how he could fulfil his promise came to him. He ran down to where the little boat lay on the shelving sand, with the ripples of the incoming tide just washing the rudder, which was still shipped. He unshipped the rudder and came back.

Under a tree, covered with the stay-sail they had brought from the *Shenandoah*, lay most of their treasures: old clothes and boots, and all the other odds and ends. The precious tobacco stitched up in a piece of canvas was there, and the housewife with the needles and threads. A hole had been dug in the sand as a sort of *cache* for them, and the stay-sail put over them to protect them from the dew.

The sun was now looking over the sea-line, and the tall cocoa-nut trees were singing and whispering together under the strengthening breeze.

XXIII

They Move Away

He began to collect the things, and carry them to the dinghy. He took the stay-sail and everything that might be useful; and when he had stowed them in the boat, he took the breaker and filled it with water at the water source in the wood; he collected some bananas and breadfruit, and stowed them in the dinghy with the breaker. Then he found the remains of yesterday's breakfast, which he had hidden between two palmetto leaves, and placed it also in the boat.

The water was now so high that a strong push would float her. He turned back to the hut for Emmeline. She was still asleep: so soundly asleep, that when he lifted her up in his arms she made no movement. He placed her carefully in the stern-sheets with her head on the sail rolled up, and then standing in the bow pushed off with a scull. Then, taking the sculls, he turned the boat's head up the lagoon to the left. He kept close to the shore, but for the life of him he could not help lifting his eyes and looking towards the reef.

Round a certain spot on the distant white coral there was a great commotion of birds. Huge birds some of them seemed, and the "Hi! hi! hi!" of them came across the lagoon on the breeze as they quarrelled together and beat the air with their wings. He turned his head away till a bend of the shore hid the spot from sight.

Here, sheltered more completely than opposite the break in the reef, the artu trees came in places right down to the water's edge; the breadfruit trees cast the shadow of their great scalloped leaves upon the water; glades, thick with fern, wildernesses of the mammee apple, and bushes of the scarlet "wild cocoa-nut" all slipped by, as the dinghy, hugging the shore, crept up the lagoon.

Gazing at the shore edge one might have imagined it the edge of a lake, but for the thunder of the Pacific upon the distant reef; and even that did not destroy the impression, but only lent a strangeness to it.

A lake in the midst of the ocean, that is what the lagoon really was.

Here and there cocoa-nut trees slanted over the water, mirroring their delicate stems, and tracing their clear-cut shadows on the sandy bottom a fathom deep below.

He kept close in-shore for the sake of the shelter of the trees. His object was to find some place where they might stop permanently, and put up a tent. He was seeking a new home, in fact. But, pretty as were the glades they passed, they were not attractive places to live in. There were too many trees, or the ferns were too deep. He was seeking air and space, and suddenly he found it. Rounding a little cape, all blazing with the scarlet of the wild cocoa-nut, the dinghy broke into a new world.

Before her lay a great sweep of the palest blue wind-swept water, down to which came a broad green sward of park-like land set on either side with deep groves, and leading up and away to higher land, where, above the massive and motionless green of the great breadfruit trees, the palm trees swayed and fluttered their pale green feathers in the breeze. The pale colour of the water was due to the extreme shallowness of the lagoon just here. So shallow was it that one could see brown spaces indicating beds of dead and rotten coral, and splashes of darkest sapphire where the deep pools lay. The reef lay more than half a mile from the shore: a great way out, it seemed, so far out that its cramping influence was removed, and one had the impression of wide and unbroken sea.

Dick rested on his oars, and let the dinghy float whilst he looked around him. He had come some four miles and a half, and this was right at the back of the island. As the boat drifting shoreward touched the bank, Emmeline awakened from her sleep, sat up, and looked around her.

BOOK II

PART I

I

Under the Artu Tree

On the edge of the green sward, between a diamond-chequered artu trunk and the massive bole of a breadfruit, a house had come into being. It was not much larger than a big hen-house, but quite sufficient for the needs of two people in a climate of eternal summer. It was built of bamboos, and thatched with a double thatch of palmetto leaves, so neatly built, and so well thatched, that one might have fancied it the production of several skilled workmen.

The breadfruit tree was barren of fruit, as these trees sometimes are, whole groves of them ceasing to bear for some mysterious reason only known to Nature. It was green now, but when suffering its yearly change the great scalloped leaves would take all imaginable tinges of gold and bronze and amber. Beyond the artu was a little clearing, where the chapparel had been carefully removed and taro roots planted.

Stepping from the house doorway on to the sward you might have fancied yourself, except for the tropical nature of the foliage, in some English park.

Looking to the right, the eye became lost in the woods, where all tints of green were tinging the foliage, and the bushes of the wild cocoa-nut burned scarlet as haw-berries.

The house had a doorway, but no door. It might have been said to have a double roof, for the breadfruit foliage above gave good shelter during the rains. Inside it was bare enough. Dried, sweet-smelling ferns covered the floor. Two sails, rolled up, lay on either side of the doorway. There was a rude shelf attached to one of the walls, and on the shelf some bowls made of cocoa-nut shell. The people to whom the place belonged evidently did not trouble it much with their presence, using it only at night, and as a refuge from the dew.

Sitting on the grass by the doorway, sheltered by the breadfruit shade, yet with the hot rays of the afternoon sun just touching her naked feet, was a girl. A girl of fifteen or sixteen, naked, except for a kilt of gaily-striped material reaching from her waist to her knees. Her long black hair was drawn back from the forehead, and tied behind with a loop of the elastic vine. A scarlet blossom was stuck behind her right ear, after the fashion of a clerk's pen. Her face was beautiful, powdered with tiny freckles; especially under the eyes, which were of a deep, tranquil blue-grey. She half sat, half lay on her left side; whilst before her, quite close, strutted up and down on the grass, a bird, with blue plumage, coral-red beak, and bright, watchful eyes.

The girl was Emmeline Lestrange. Just by her elbow stood a little bowl made from half a cocoa-nut, and filled with some white substance with which she was feeding the bird. Dick had found it in the woods two years ago, quite small, deserted by its mother, and starving. They had fed it and tamed it, and it was now one of the family; roosting on the roof at night, and appearing regularly at meal times.

All at once she held out her hand; the bird flew into the air, lit on her forefinger and balanced itself, sinking its head between its shoulders, and uttering the sound which formed its entire vocabulary and one means of vocal expression—a sound from which it had derived its name.

"Koko," said Emmeline, "where is Dick?"

The bird turned his head about, as if he were searching for his master; and the girl lay back lazily on the grass, laughing, and holding him up poised on her finger, as if he were some enamelled jewel she wished to admire at a little distance. They made a pretty picture under the cave-like shadow of the breadfruit leaves; and it was difficult to understand how this young girl, so perfectly formed, so fully developed, and so beautiful, had evolved from plain little Emmeline Lestrange. And the whole thing, as far as the beauty of her was concerned, had happened during the last six months.

II

HALF CHILD—HALF SAVAGE

Five rainy seasons had passed and gone since the tragic occurrence on the reef. Five long years the breakers had thundered, and the sea-gulls had cried round the figure whose spell had drawn a mysterious barrier across the lagoon.

The children had never returned to the old place. They had kept entirely to the back of the island and the woods—the lagoon, down to a certain point, and the reef; a wide enough and beautiful enough world, but a hopeless world, as far as help from civilisation was concerned. For, of the few ships that touched at the island in the course of years, how many would explore the lagoon or woods? Perhaps not one.

Occasionally Dick would make an excursion in the dinghy to the old place, but Emmeline refused to accompany him. He went chiefly to obtain bananas; for on the whole island there was but one clump of banana trees—that near the water source in the wood, where the old green skulls had been discovered, and the little barrel.

She had never quite recovered from the occurrence on the reef. Something had been shown to her, the purport of which she vaguely understood, and it had filled her with horror and a terror of the place where it had occurred. Dick was quite different. He had been frightened enough at first; but the feeling wore away in time.

Dick had built three houses in succession during the five years. He had laid out a patch of taro and another of sweet potatoes. He knew every pool on the reef for two miles either way, and the forms of their inhabitants; and though he did not know the names of the creatures to be found there, he made a profound study of their habits.

He had seen some astonishing things during these five years—from a fight between a whale and two thrashers conducted outside the reef, lasting an hour, and dyeing the breaking waves with blood, to the poisoning of the fish in the lagoon by fresh water, due to an extraordinarily heavy rainy season.

He knew the woods of the back of the island by heart, and the forms of life that inhabited them—butterflies, and moths, and birds, lizards, and insects of strange shape; extraordinary orchids—some filthy-looking, the very image of corruption, some beautiful, and all strange. He found melons and guavas, and breadfruit, the red apple of Tahiti, and the great Brazilian plum, taro in plenty, and a dozen other good things—but there were no bananas. This made him unhappy at times, for he was human.

Though Emmeline had asked Koko for Dick's whereabouts, it was only a remark made by way of making conversation, for she could hear him in the little cane-brake which lay close by amidst the trees.

In a few minutes he appeared, dragging after him two canes which he had just cut, and wiping the perspiration off his brow with his naked arm. He had an old pair of trousers on—part of the truck salved long ago from the *Shenandoah*—nothing else, and he was well worth looking at and considering, both from a physical and psychological point of view.

Auburn-haired and tall, looking more like seventeen than sixteen, with a restless and daring expression, half a child, half a man, half a civilised being, half a savage, he had both progressed and retrograded during the five years of savage life. He sat down beside Emmeline, flung the canes beside him, tried the edge of the old butcher's knife with which he had cut them, then, taking one of the canes across his knee, he began whittling at it.

"What are you making?" asked Emmeline, releasing the bird, which flew into one of the branches of the artu and rested there, a blue point amidst the dark green.

"Fish-spear," replied Dick.

Without being taciturn, he rarely wasted words. Life was all business for him. He would talk to Emmeline, but always in short sentences; and he had developed the habit of talking to inanimate things, to the fish-spear he was carving, or the bowl he was fashioning from a cocoa-nut.

As for Emmeline, even as a child she had never been talkative. There was something mysterious in her personality, something secretive. Her mind seemed half submerged in twilight. Though she spoke little, and though the subject of their conversations was almost entirely material and relative to their everyday needs, her mind would wander into abstract fields and the land of chimerae and dreams. What she found there no one knew—least of all, perhaps, herself.

As for Dick, he would sometimes talk and mutter to himself, as if in a reverie; but if you caught the words, you would find that they referred to no abstraction, but to some trifle he had on hand. He seemed entirely

HENRY DE VERE STACPOOLE

bound up in the moment, and to have forgotten the past as completely as though it had never been.

Yet he had his contemplative moods. He would lie with his face over a rock-pool by the hour, watching the strange forms of life to be seen there, or sit in the woods motionless as a stone, watching the birds and the swift-slipping lizards. The birds came so close that he could easily have knocked them over, but he never hurt one or interfered in anyway with the wild life of the woods.

The island, the lagoon, and the reef were for him the three volumes of a great picture book, as they were for Emmeline, though in a different manner. The colour and the beauty of it all fed some mysterious want in her soul. Her life was a long reverie, a beautiful vision—troubled with shadows. Across all the blue and coloured spaces that meant months and years she could still see as in a glass dimly the *Northumberland*, smoking against the wild background of fog; her uncle's face, Boston—a vague and dark picture beyond a storm—and nearer, the tragic form on the reef that still haunted terribly her dreams. But she never spoke of these things to Dick. Just as she kept the secret of what was in her box, and the secret of her trouble whenever she lost it, she kept the secret of her feelings about these things.

Born of these things there remained with her always a vague terror: the terror of losing Dick. Mrs. Stannard, her uncle, the dim people she had known in Boston, all had passed away out of her life like a dream and shadows. The other one too, most horribly. What if Dick were taken from her as well?

This haunting trouble had been with her a long time; up to a few months ago it had been mainly personal and selfish—the dread of being left alone. But lately it had altered and become more acute. Dick had changed in her eyes, and the fear was now for him. Her own personality had suddenly and strangely become merged in his. The idea of life without him was unthinkable, yet the trouble remained, a menace in the blue.

Some days it would be worse than others. Today, for instance, it was worse than yesterday, as though some danger had crept close to them during the night. Yet the sky and sea were stainless, the sun shone on tree and flower, the west wind brought the tune of the far-away reef like a lullaby. There was nothing to hint of danger or the need of distrust.

At last Dick finished his spear and rose to his feet.

"Where are you going?" asked Emmeline.

"The reef," he replied. "The tide's going out."

"I'll go with you," said she.

He went into the house and stowed the precious knife away. Then he came out, spear in one hand, and half a fathom of liana in the other. The liana was for the purpose of stringing the fish on, should the catch be large. He led the way down the grassy sward to the lagoon where the dinghy lay, close up to the bank, and moored to a post driven into the soft soil. Emmeline got in, and, taking the sculls, he pushed off. The tide was going out.

I have said that the reef just here lay a great way out from the shore. The lagoon was so shallow that at low tide one could have waded almost right across it, were it not for pot-holes here and there—ten-feet traps—and great beds of rotten coral, into which one would sink as into brushwood, to say nothing of the nettle coral that stings like a bed of nettles. There were also other dangers. Tropical shallows are full of wild surprises in the way of life—and death.

Dick had long ago marked out in his memory the soundings of the lagoon, and it was fortunate that he possessed the special sense of location which is the main stand-by of the hunter and the savage, for, from the disposition of the coral in ribs, the water from the shore edge to the reef ran in lanes. Only two of these lanes gave a clear, fair way from the shore edge to the reef; had you followed the others, even in a boat of such shallow draught as the dinghy, you would have found yourself stranded half-way across, unless, indeed, it were a spring tide.

Half-way across the sound of the surf on the barrier became louder, and the everlasting and monotonous cry of the gulls came on the breeze. It was lonely out here, and, looking back, the shore seemed a great way off. It was lonelier still on the reef.

Dick tied up the boat to a projection of coral, and helped Emmeline to land. The sun was creeping down into the west, the tide was nearly half out, and large pools of water lay glittering like burnished shields in the sunlight. Dick, with his precious spear beside him, sat calmly down on a ledge of coral, and began to divest himself of his one and only garment.

Emmeline turned away her head and contemplated the distant shore, which seemed thrice as far off as it was in reality. When she turned her head again he was racing along the edge of the surf. He and his spear silhouetted against the spindrift and dazzling foam formed a picture savage enough, and well in keeping with the general desolation

HENRY DE VERE STACPOOLE

of the background. She watched him lie down and cling to a piece of coral, whilst the surf rushed round and over him, and then rise and shake himself like a dog, and pursue his gambols, his body all glittering with the wet.

Sometimes a whoop would come on the breeze, mixing with the sound of the surf and the cry of the gulls, and she would see him plunge his spear into a pool, and the next moment the spear would be held aloft with something struggling and glittering at the end of it.

He was quite different out here on the reef to what he was ashore. The surroundings here seemed to develop all that was savage in him, in a startling way; and he would kill, and kill, just for the pleasure of killing, destroying more fish than they could possibly use.

III

The Demon of the Reef

The romance of coral has still to be written. There still exists a widespread opinion that the coral reef and the coral island are the work of an "insect." This fabulous insect, accredited with the genius of Brunel and the patience of Job, has been humorously enough held up before the children of many generations as an example of industry—a thing to be admired, a model to be followed.

As a matter of fact, nothing could be more slothful or slow, more given up to a life of ease and degeneracy, than the "reef-building polypifer"—to give him his scientific name. He is the hobo of the animal world, but, unlike the hobo, he does not even tramp for a living. He exists as a sluggish and gelatinous worm; he attracts to himself calcareous elements from the water to make himself a house—mark you, the sea does the building—he dies, and he leaves his house behind him—and a reputation for industry, beside which the reputation of the ant turns pale, and that of the bee becomes of little account.

On a coral reef you are treading on rock that the reef-building polypifers of ages have left behind them as evidences of their idle and apparently useless lives. You might fancy that the reef is formed of dead rock, but it is not: that is where the wonder of the thing comes in—a coral reef is half alive. If it were not, it would not resist the action of the sea ten years. The live part of the reef is just where the breakers come in and beyond. The gelatinous rock-building polypifers die almost at once, if exposed to the sun or if left uncovered by water.

Sometimes, at very low tide, if you have courage enough to risk being swept away by the breakers, going as far out on the reef as you can, you may catch a glimpse of them in their living state—great mounds and masses of what seems rock, but which is a honeycomb of coral, whose cells are filled with the living polypifers. Those in the uppermost cells are usually dead, but lower down they are living.

Always dying, always being renewed, devoured by fish, attacked by the sea—that is the life of a coral reef. It is a thing as living as a cabbage or a tree. Every storm tears a piece off the reef, which the living

HENRY DE VERE STACPOOLE

coral replaces; wounds occur in it which actually granulate and heal as wounds do of the human body.

There is nothing, perhaps, more mysterious in nature than this fact of the existence of a living land: a land that repairs itself, when injured, by vital processes, and resists the eternal attack of the sea by vital force, especially when we think of the extent of some of these lagoon islands or atolls, whose existences are an eternal battle with the waves.

Unlike the island of this story (which is an island surrounded by a barrier reef of coral surrounding a space of sea—the lagoon), the reef forms the island. The reef may be grown over by trees, or it may be perfectly destitute of important vegetation, or it may be crusted with islets. Some islets may exist within the lagoon, but as often as not it is just a great empty lake floored with sand and coral, peopled with life different to the life of the outside ocean, protected from the waves, and reflecting the sky like a mirror.

When we remember that the atoll is a living thing, an organic whole, as full of life, though not so highly organised, as a tortoise, the meanest imagination must be struck with the immensity of one of the structures.

Vliegen atoll in the Low Archipelago, measured from lagoon edge to lagoon edge, is sixty miles long by twenty miles broad, at its broadest part. In the Marshall Archipelago, Rimsky Korsacoff is fifty-four miles long and twenty miles broad; and Rimsky Korsacoff is a living thing, secreting, excreting, and growing—more highly organised than the cocoa-nut trees that grow upon its back, or the blossoms that powder the hotoo trees in its groves.

The story of coral is the story of a world, and the longest chapter in that story concerns itself with coral's infinite variety and form.

Out on the margin of the reef where Dick was spearing fish, you might have seen a peach-blossom-coloured lichen on the rock. This lichen was a form of coral. Coral growing upon coral, and in the pools at the edge of the surf branching corals also of the colour of a peach bloom.

Within a hundred yards of where Emmeline was sitting, the pools contained corals of all colours, from lake-red to pure white, and the lagoon behind her—corals of the quaintest and strangest forms.

Dick had speared several fish, and had left them lying on the reef to be picked up later on. Tired of killing, he was now wandering along, examining the various living things he came across.

Huge slugs inhabited the reef, slugs as big as parsnips, and somewhat of the same shape; they were a species of Bech de mer. Globe-shaped jelly-fish as big as oranges, great cuttlefish bones flat and shining and white, shark's teeth, spines of echini; sometimes a dead scarus fish, its stomach distended with bits of coral on which it had been feeding; crabs, sea urchins, sea-weeds of strange colour and shape; star-fish, some tiny and of the colour of cayenne pepper, some huge and pale. These and a thousand other things, beautiful or strange, were to be found on the reef.

Dick had laid his spear down, and was exploring a deep bath-like pool. He had waded up to his knees, and was in the act of wading further when he was suddenly seized by the foot. It was just as if his ankle had been suddenly caught in a clove hitch and the rope drawn tight. He screamed out with pain and terror, and suddenly and viciously a whip-lash shot out from the water, lassoed him round the left knee, drew itself taut, and held him.

IV

What Beauty Concealed

Emmeline, seated on the coral rock, had almost forgotten Dick for a moment. The sun was setting, and the warm amber light of the sunset shone on reef and rock-pool. Just at sunset and low tide the reef had a peculiar fascination for her. It had the low-tide smell of sea-weed exposed to the air, and the torment and trouble of the breakers seemed eased. Before her, and on either side, the foam-dashed coral glowed in amber and gold, and the great Pacific came glassing and glittering in, voiceless and peaceful, till it reached the strand and burst into song and spray.

Here, just as on the hill-top at the other side of the island, you could mark the rhythm of the rollers. "Forever, and forever—forever, and forever," they seemed to say.

The cry of the gulls came mixed with the spray on the breeze. They haunted the reef like uneasy spirits, always complaining, never at rest; but at sunset their cry seemed farther away and less melancholy, perhaps because just then the whole island world seemed bathed in the spirit of peace.

She turned from the sea prospect and looked backwards over the lagoon to the island. She could make out the broad green glade beside which their little house lay, and a spot of yellow, which was the thatch of the house, just by the artu tree, and nearly hidden by the shadow of the breadfruit. Over woods the fronds of the great cocoa-nut palms showed above every other tree silhouetted against the dim, dark blue of the eastern sky.

Seen by the enchanted light of sunset, the whole picture had an unreal look, more lovely than a dream. At dawn—and Dick would often start for the reef before dawn, if the tide served—the picture was as beautiful; more so, perhaps, for over the island, all in shadow, and against the stars, you would see the palm-tops catching fire, and then the light of day coming through the green trees and blue sky, like a spirit, across the blue lagoon, widening and strengthening as it widened, across the white foam, out over the sea, spreading like a fan, till, all at once, night was day, and the gulls were crying and the breakers flashing, the dawn wind blowing, and the palm trees bending, as palm trees only know how. Emmeline always imagined herself alone on the island with Dick, but beauty was there, too, and beauty is a great companion.

The girl was contemplating the scene before her. Nature in her friendliest mood seemed to say, "Behold me! Men call me cruel; men have called me deceitful, even treacherous. *I*—ah well! my answer is, 'Behold me!'"

The girl was contemplating the specious beauty of it all, when on the breeze from seaward came a shout. She turned quickly. There was Dick up to his knees in a rock-pool a hundred yards or so away, motionless, his arms upraised, and crying out for help. She sprang to her feet.

There had once been an islet on this part of the reef, a tiny thing, consisting of a few palms and a handful of vegetation, and destroyed, perhaps, in some great storm. I mention this because the existence of this islet once upon a time was the means, indirectly, of saving Dick's life; for where these islets have been or are, "flats" occur on the reef formed of coral conglomerate.

Emmeline in her bare feet could never have reached him in time over rough coral, but, fortunately, this flat and comparatively smooth surface lay between them.

"My spear!" shouted Dick, as she approached.

He seemed at first tangled in brambles; then she thought ropes were tangling round him and tying him to something in the water—whatever it was, it was most awful, and hideous, and like a nightmare. She ran with the speed of Atalanta to the rock where the spear was resting, all red with the blood of new-slain fish, a foot from the point.

As she approached Dick, spear in hand, she saw, gasping with terror, that the ropes were alive, and that they were flickering and rippling over his back. One of them bound his left arm to his side, but his right arm was free.

"Quick!" he shouted.

In a second the spear was in his free hand, and Emmeline had cast herself down on her knees, and was staring with terrified eyes into the water of the pool from whence the ropes issued. She was, despite her terror, quite prepared to fling herself in and do battle with the thing, whatever it might be.

What she saw was only for a second. In the deep water of the pool, gazing up and forward and straight at Dick, she saw a face, lugubrious and awful. The eyes were wide as saucers, stony and steadfast; a large, heavy, parrot-like beak hung before the eyes, and worked and wobbled, and seemed to beckon. But what froze one's heart was the expression of the eyes, so stony and lugubrious, so passionless, so devoid of speculation, yet so fixed of purpose and full of fate.

From away far down he had risen with the rising tide. He had been feeding on crabs, when the tide, betraying him, had gone out, leaving him trapped in the rock-pool. He had slept, perhaps, and awakened to find a being, naked and defenceless, invading his pool. He was quite small, as octopods go, and young, yet he was large and powerful enough to have drowned an ox.

The octopod has only been described once, in stone, by a Japanese artist. The statue is still extant, and it is the most terrible masterpiece of sculpture ever executed by human hands. It represents a man who has been bathing on a low-tide beach, and has been caught. The man is shouting in a delirium of terror, and threatening with his free arm the spectre that has him in its grip. The eyes of the octopod are fixed upon the man—passionless and lugubrious eyes, but steadfast and fixed.

Another whip-lash shot out of the water in a shower of spray, and seized Dick by the left thigh. At the same instant he drove the point of the spear through the right eye of the monster, deep down through eye and soft gelatinous carcass till the spear-point dirled and splintered against the rock. At the same moment the water of the pool became black as ink, the bands around him relaxed, and he was free.

Emmeline rose up and seized him, sobbing and clinging to him, and kissing him. He clasped her with his left arm round her body, as if to protect her, but it was a mechanical action. He was not thinking of her. Wild with rage, and uttering hoarse cries, he plunged the broken spear again and again into the depths of the pool, seeking utterly to destroy the enemy that had so lately had him in its grip. Then slowly he came to himself, and wiped his forehead, and looked at the broken spear in his hand.

"Beast!" he said. "Did you see its eyes? Did you see its eyes? I wish it had a hundred eyes, and I had a hundred spears to drive into them!"

She was clinging to him, and sobbing and laughing hysterically, and praising him. One might have thought that he had rescued her from death, not she him.

The sun had nearly vanished, and he led her back to where the dinghy was moored recapturing and putting on his trousers on the road. He picked up the dead fish he had speared; and as he rowed her back across the lagoon, he talked and laughed, recounting the incidents of the fight, taking all the glory of the thing to himself, and seeming quite to ignore the important part she had played in it.

This was not from any callousness or want of gratitude, but simply from the fact that for the last five years he had been the be-all and end-all of their tiny community—the Imperial master. And he would just as soon have thought of thanking her for handing him the spear as of thanking his right hand for driving it home. She was quite content, seeking neither thanks nor praise. Everything she had came from him: she was his shadow and his slave. He was her sun.

He went over the fight again and again before they lay down to rest, telling her he had done this and that, and what he would do to the next beast of the sort. The reiteration was tiresome enough, or would have been to an outside listener, but to Emmeline it was better than Homer. People's minds do not improve in an intellectual sense when they are isolated from the world, even though they are living the wild and happy lives of savages.

Then Dick lay down in the dried ferns and covered himself with a piece of the striped flannel which they used for blanketing, and he snored, and chattered in his sleep like a dog hunting imaginary game, and Emmeline lay beside him wakeful and thinking. A new terror had come into her life. She had seen death for the second time, but this time active and in being.

V

The Sound of a Drum

The next day Dick was sitting under the shade of the artu. He had the box of fishhooks beside him, and he was bending a line on to one of them. There had originally been a couple of dozen hooks, large and small, in the box; there remained now only six—four small and two large ones. It was a large one he was fixing to the line, for he intended going on the morrow to the old place to fetch some bananas, and on the way to try for a fish in the deeper parts of the lagoon.

It was late afternoon, and the heat had gone out of the day. Emmeline, seated on the grass opposite to him, was holding the end of the line, whilst he got the kinks out of it, when suddenly she raised her head.

There was not a breath of wind; the hush of the far-distant surf came through the blue weather—the only audible sound except, now and then, a movement and flutter from the bird perched in the branches of the artu. All at once another sound mixed itself with the voice of the surf—a faint, throbbing sound, like the beating of a distant drum.

"Listen!" said Emmeline.

Dick paused for a moment in his work. All the sounds of the island were familiar: this was something quite strange.

Faint and far away, now rapid, now slow, coming from where, who could say? Sometimes it seemed to come from the sea, sometimes, if the fancy of the listener turned that way, from the woods. As they listened, a sigh came from overhead; the evening breeze had risen and was moving in the leaves of the artu tree. Just as you might wipe a picture off a slate, the breeze banished the sound. Dick went on with his work.

Next morning early he embarked in the dinghy. He took the hook and line with him, and some raw fish for bait. Emmeline helped him to push off, and stood on the bank waving her hand as he rounded the little cape covered with wild cocoa-nut.

These expeditions of Dick's were one of her sorrows. To be left alone was frightful; yet she never complained. She was living in a paradise, but something told her that behind all that sun, all that splendour of blue sea and sky, behind the flowers and the leaves, behind all that specious and simpering appearance of happiness in nature, lurked a frown, and the dragon of mischance.

Dick rowed for about a mile, then he shipped his sculls, and let the dinghy float. The water here was very deep; so deep that, despite its clearness, the bottom was invisible; the sunlight over the reef struck through it diagonally, filling it with sparkles.

The fisherman baited his hook with a piece from the belly of a scarus and lowered it down out of sight, then he belayed the line to a thole pin, and, sitting in the bottom of the boat, hung his head over the side and gazed deep down into the water. Sometimes there was nothing to see but just the deep blue of the water. Then a flight of spangled arrowheads would cross the line of sight and vanish, pursued by a form like a moving bar of gold. Then a great fish would materialise itself and hang in the shadow of the boat motionless as a stone, save for the movement of its gills; next moment with a twist of the tail it would be gone.

Suddenly the dinghy shored over, and might have capsized, only for the fact that Dick was sitting on the opposite side to the side from which the line hung. Then the boat righted; the line slackened, and the surface of the lagoon, a few fathoms away, boiled as if being stirred from below by a great silver stick. He had hooked an albicore. He tied the end of the fishing-line to a scull, undid the line from the thole pin, and flung the scull overboard.

He did all this with wonderful rapidity, while the line was still slack. Next moment the scull was rushing over the surface of the lagoon, now towards the reef, now towards the shore, now flat, now end up. Now it would be jerked under the surface entirely; vanish for a moment, and then reappear. It was a most astonishing thing to watch, for the scull seemed alive—viciously alive, and imbued with some destructive purpose; as, in fact, it was. The most venomous of living things, and the most intelligent could not have fought the great fish better.

The albicore would make a frantic dash down the lagoon, hoping, perhaps, to find in the open sea a release from his foe. Then, half drowned with the pull of the scull, he would pause, dart from side to side in perplexity, and then make an equally frantic dash up the lagoon, to be checked in the same manner. Seeking the deepest depths, he would sink the scull a few fathoms; and once he sought the air, leaping into the sunlight like a crescent of silver, whilst the splash of him as he fell echoed amidst the trees bordering the lagoon. An hour passed before the great fish showed signs of weakening.

The struggle had taken place up to this close to the shore, but now the scull swam out into the broad sheet of sunlit water, and slowly began to describe large circles rippling up the peaceful blue into flashing wavelets. It was a melancholy sight to watch, for the great fish had made a good fight, and one could see him, through the eye of imagination, beaten, half drowned, dazed, and moving as is the fashion of dazed things in a circle.

Dick, working the remaining oar at the stern of the boat, rowed out and seized the floating scull, bringing it on board. Foot by foot he hauled his catch towards the boat till the long gleaming line of the thing came dimly into view.

The fight had been heard for miles through the lagoon water by all sorts of swimming things. The lord of the place had got sound of it. A dark fin rippled the water; and as Dick, pulling on his line, hauled his catch closer, a monstrous grey shadow stained the depths, and the glittering streak that was the albicore vanished as if engulfed in a cloud. The line came in slack, and Dick hauled in the albicore's head. It had been divided from the body as if with a huge pair of shears. The grey shadow slipped by the boat, and Dick, mad with rage, shouted and shook his fist at it; then, seizing the albicore's head, from which he had taken the hook, he hurled it at the monster in the water.

The great shark, with a movement of the tail that caused the water to swirl and the dinghy to rock, turned upon his back and engulfed the head; then he slowly sank and vanished, just as if he had been dissolved. He had come off best in this their first encounter—such as it was.

VI

SAILS UPON THE SEA

Dick put the hook away and took to the sculls. He had a three-mile row before him, and the tide was coming in, which did not make it any the easier. As he rowed, he talked and grumbled to himself. He had been in a grumbling mood for sometime past: the chief cause, Emmeline.

In the last few months she had changed; even her face had changed. A new person had come upon the island, it seemed to him, and taken the place of the Emmeline he had known from earliest childhood. This one looked different. He did not know that she had grown beautiful, he just knew that she looked different; also she had developed new ways that displeased him—she would go off and bathe by herself, for instance.

Up to six months or so ago he had been quite contented; sleeping and eating, and hunting for food and cooking it, building and rebuilding the house, exploring the woods and the reef. But lately a spirit of restlessness had come upon him; he did not know exactly what he wanted. He had a vague feeling that he wanted to go away from the place where he was; not from the island, but from the place where they had pitched their tent, or rather built their house.

It may have been the spirit of civilisation crying out in him, telling him of all he was missing. Of the cities, and the streets, and the houses, and the businesses, and the striving after gold, the striving after power. It may have been simply the man in him crying out for Love, and not knowing yet that Love was at his elbow.

The dinghy glided along, hugging the shore, past the little glades of fern and the cathedral gloom of the breadfruit; then, rounding a promontory, she opened the view of the break in the reef. A little bit of the white strand was visible, but he was not looking that way—he was looking towards the reef at a tiny, dark spot, not noticeable unless searched for by the eye. Always when he came on these expeditions, just here, he would hang on his oars and gaze over there, where the gulls were flying and the breakers thundering.

A few years ago the spot filled him with dread as well as curiosity, but from familiarity and the dullness that time casts on everything, the dread had almost vanished, but the curiosity remained: the curiosity that makes a child look on at the slaughter of an animal even though his soul revolts at it. He gazed for a while, then he went on pulling, and the dinghy approached the beach.

Something had happened on the beach. The sand was all trampled, and stained red here and there; in the centre lay the remains of a great fire still smouldering, and just where the water lapped the sand, lay two deep grooves as if two heavy boats had been beached there. A South Sea man would have told from the shape of the grooves, and the little marks of the out-riggers, that two heavy canoes had been beached there. And they had.

The day before, early in the afternoon, two canoes, possibly from that far-away island which cast a stain on the horizon to the sou'-sou'-west, had entered the lagoon, one in pursuit of the other.

What happened then had better be left veiled. A war drum with a shark-skin head had set the woods throbbing; the victory was celebrated all night, and at dawn the victors manned the two canoes and set sail for the home, or the hell, they had come from. Had you examined the strand you would have found that a line had been drawn across the beach, beyond which there were no footmarks: that meant that the rest of the island was for some reason *tabu*.

Dick pulled the nose of the boat up a bit on the strand, then he looked around him. He picked up a broken spear that had been cast away or forgotten; it was made of some hard wood and barbed with iron. On the right-hand side of the beach something lay between the cocoa-nut trees. He approached; it was a mass of offal; the entrails of a dozen sheep seemed cast here in one mound, yet there were no sheep on the island, and sheep are not carried as a rule in war canoes.

The sand on the beach was eloquent. The foot pursuing and the foot pursued; the knee of the fallen one, and then the forehead and outspread hands; the heel of the chief who has slain his enemy, beaten the body flat, burst a hole through it through which he has put his head, and who stands absolutely wearing his enemy as a cloak; the head of the man dragged on his back to be butchered like a sheep—of these things spoke the sand.

As far as the sand traces could speak, the story of the battle was still being told; the screams and the shouting, the clashing of clubs and spears were gone, yet the ghost of the fight remained.

If the sand could bear such traces, and tell such tales, who shall say that the plastic æther was destitute of the story of the fight and the butchery?

However that may have been, Dick, looking around him, had the shivering sense of having just escaped from danger. Whoever had been, had gone—he could tell that by the canoe traces. Gone either out to sea, or up the right stretch of the lagoon. It was important to determine this.

He climbed to the hill-top and swept the sea with his eyes. There, away to the south-west, far away on the sea, he could distinguish the brown sails of two canoes. There was something indescribably mournful and lonely in their appearance; they looked like withered leaves—brown moths blown to sea—derelicts of autumn. Then, remembering the beach, these things became freighted with the most sinister thoughts for the mind of the gazer. They were hurrying away, having done their work. That they looked lonely and old and mournful, and like withered leaves blown across the sea, only heightened the horror.

Dick had never seen canoes before, but he knew that these things were boats of some sort holding people, and that the people had left all those traces on the beach. How much of the horror of the thing was revealed to his subconscious intelligence, who can say?

He had climbed the boulder, and he now sat down with his knees drawn up, and his hands clasped round them. Whenever he came round to this side of the island, something happened of a fateful or sinister nature. The last time he had nearly lost the dinghy; he had beached the little boat in such a way that she floated off, and the tide was just in the act of stealing her, and sweeping her from the lagoon out to sea, when he returned laden with his bananas, and, rushing into the water up to his waist, saved her. Another time he had fallen out of a tree, and just by a miracle escaped death. Another time a hurricane had broken, lashing the lagoon into snow, and sending the cocoa-nuts bounding and flying like tennis balls across the strand. This time he had just escaped something, he knew not exactly what. It was almost as if Providence were saying to him, "Don't come here."

He watched the brown sails as they dwindled in the wind-blown blue, then he came down from the hill-top and cut his bananas. He cut four large bunches, which caused him to make two journeys to the boat. When the bananas were stowed he pushed off.

For a long time a great curiosity had been pulling at his heart-strings: a curiosity of which he was dimly ashamed. Fear had given it birth, and Fear still clung to it. It was, perhaps, the element of fear and the awful delight of daring the unknown that made him give way to it.

He had rowed, perhaps, a hundred yards when he turned the boat's head and made for the reef. It was more than five years since that day when he rowed across the lagoon, Emmeline sitting in the stern, with her wreath of flowers in her hand. It might have been only yesterday, for everything seemed just the same. The thunderous surf and the flying gulls, the blinding sunlight, and the salt, fresh smell of the sea. The palm tree at the entrance of the lagoon still bent gazing into the water, and round the projection of coral to which he had last moored the boat still lay a fragment of the rope which he had cut in his hurry to escape.

Ships had come into the lagoon, perhaps, during the five years, but no one had noticed anything on the reef, for it was only from the hill-top that a full view of what was there could be seen, and then only by eyes knowing where to look. From the beach there was visible just a speck. It might have been, perhaps, a bit of old wreckage flung there by a wave in some big storm. A piece of old wreckage that had been tossed hither and thither for years, and had at last found a place of rest.

Dick tied the boat up, and stepped on to the reef. It was high tide just as before; the breeze was blowing strongly, and overhead a man-of-war's bird, black as ebony, with a blood-red bill, came sailing, the wind doming out his wings. He circled in the air, and cried out fiercely, as if resenting the presence of the intruder, then he passed away, let himself be blown away, as it were, across the lagoon, wheeled, circled, and passed out to sea.

Dick approached the place he knew, and there lay the little old barrel all warped by the powerful sun; the staves stood apart, and the hooping was rusted and broken, and whatever it had contained in the way of spirit and conviviality had long ago drained away.

Beside the barrel lay a skeleton, round which lay a few rags of cloth. The skull had fallen to one side, and the lower jaw had fallen from the skull; the bones of the hands and feet were still articulated, and the ribs had not fallen in. It was all white and bleached, and the sun shone on it as indifferently as on the coral, this shell and framework that had once been a man. There was nothing dreadful about it, but a whole world of wonder.

To Dick, who had not been broken into the idea of death, who had not learned to associate it with graves and funerals, sorrow, eternity, and hell, the thing spoke as it never could have spoken to you or me.

Looking at it, things linked themselves together in his mind: the skeletons of birds he had found in the woods, the fish he had slain, even trees lying dead and rotten—even the shells of crabs.

If you had asked him what lay before him, and if he could have expressed the thought in his mind, he would have answered you "change."

All the philosophy in the world could not have told him more than he knew just then about death—he, who even did not know its name.

He was held spellbound by the marvel and miracle of the thing and the thoughts that suddenly crowded his mind like a host of spectres for whom a door has just been opened.

Just as a child by unanswerable logic knows that a fire which has burned him once will burn him again, or will burn another person, he knew that just as the form before him was, his form would be some day—and Emmeline's.

Then came the vague question which is born not of the brain, but the heart, and which is the basis of all religions—where shall I be then? His mind was not of an introspective nature, and the question just strayed across it and was gone. And still the wonder of the thing held him. He was for the first time in his life in a reverie; the corpse that had shocked and terrified him five years ago had cast seeds of thought with its dead fingers upon his mind, the skeleton had brought them to maturity. The full fact of universal death suddenly appeared before him, and he recognised it.

He stood for a long time motionless, and then with a deep sigh turned to the boat and pushed off without once looking back at the reef. He crossed the lagoon and rowed slowly homewards, keeping in the shelter of the tree shadows as much as possible.

Even looking at him from the shore you might have noticed a difference in him. Your savage paddles his canoe, or sculls his boat, alert, glancing about him, at touch with nature at all points; though he be lazy as a cat and sleeps half the day, awake he is all ears and eyes—a creature reacting to the least external impression.

Dick, as he rowed back, did not look about him: he was thinking or retrospecting. The savage in him had received a check. As he turned the little cape where the wild cocoa-nut blazed, he looked over his shoulder. A figure was standing on the sward by the edge of the water. It was Emmeline.

VII

The Schooner

They carried the bananas up to the house, and hung them from a branch of the artu. Then Dick, on his knees, lit the fire to prepare the evening meal. When it was over he went down to where the boat was moored, and returned with something in his hand. It was the javelin with the iron point—or, rather, the two pieces of it. He had said nothing of what he had seen to the girl.

Emmeline was seated on the grass; she had a long strip of the striped flannel stuff about her, worn like a scarf, and she had another piece in her hand which she was hemming. The bird was hopping about, pecking at a banana which they had thrown to him; a light breeze made the shadow of the artu leaves dance upon the grass, and the serrated leaves of the breadfruit to patter one on the other with the sound of rain-drops falling upon glass.

"Where did you get it?" asked Emmeline, staring at the piece of the javelin which Dick had flung down almost beside her whilst he went into the house to fetch the knife.

"It was on the beach over there," he replied, taking his seat and examining the two fragments to see how he could splice them together.

Emmeline looked at the pieces, putting them together in her mind. She did not like the look of the thing: so keen and savage, and stained dark a foot and more from the point.

"People had been there," said Dick, putting the two pieces together and examining the fracture critically.

"Where?"

"Over there. This was lying on the sand, and the sand was all trod up."

"Dick," said Emmeline, "who were the people?"

"I don't know; I went up the hill and saw their boats going away—far away out. This was lying on the sand."

"Dick," said Emmeline, "do you remember the noise yesterday?"

"Yes," said Dick.

"I heard it in the night."

"When?"

"In the night before the moon went away."

"That was them," said Dick.

"Dick!"

"Yes?"

"Who were they?"

"I don't know," replied Dick.

"It was in the night, before the moon went away, and it went on and on beating in the trees. I thought I was asleep, and then I knew I was awake; you were asleep, and I pushed you to listen, but you couldn't wake, you were so asleep; then the moon went away, and the noise went on. How did they make the noise?"

"I don't know," replied Dick, "but it was them; and they left this on the sand, and the sand was all trod up, and I saw their boats from the hill, away out far."

"I thought I heard voices," said Emmeline, "but I was not sure."

She fell into meditation, watching her companion at work on the savage and sinister-looking thing in his hands. He was splicing the two pieces together with a strip of the brown cloth-like stuff which is wrapped round the stalks of the cocoa-palm fronds. The thing seemed to have been hurled here out of the blue by some unseen hand.

When he had spliced the pieces, doing so with marvellous dexterity, he took the thing short down near the point, and began thrusting it into the soft earth to clean it; then, with a bit of flannel, he polished it till it shone. He felt a keen delight in it. It was useless as a fish-spear, because it had no barb, but it was a weapon. It was useless as a weapon, because there was no foe on the island to use it against; still, it was a weapon.

When he had finished scrubbing at it, he rose, hitched his old trousers up, tightened the belt of cocoa-cloth which Emmeline had made for him, went into the house and got his fish-spear, and stalked off to the boat, calling out to Emmeline to follow him. They crossed over to the reef, where, as usual, he divested himself of clothing.

It was strange that out here he would go about stark naked, yet on the island he always wore some covering. But not so strange, perhaps, after all.

The sea is a great purifier, both of the mind and the body; before that great sweet spirit people do not think in the same way as they think far inland. What woman would appear in a town or on a country road, or even bathing in a river, as she appears bathing in the sea?

Some instinct made Dick cover himself up on shore, and strip naked on the reef. In a minute he was down by the edge of the surf, javelin in one hand, fish-spear in the other.

HENRY DE VERE STACPOOLE

Emmeline, by a little pool the bottom of which was covered with branching coral, sat gazing down into its depths, lost in a reverie like that into which we fall when gazing at shapes in the fire. She had sat sometime like this when a shout from Dick aroused her. She started to her feet and gazed to where he was pointing. An amazing thing was there.

To the east, just rounding the curve of the reef, and scarcely a quarter of a mile from it, was coming a big topsail schooner; a beautiful sight she was, heeling to the breeze with every sail drawing, and the white foam like a feather at her fore-foot.

Dick, with the javelin in his hand, was standing gazing at her; he had dropped his fish-spear, and he stood as motionless as though he were carved out of stone. Emmeline ran to him and stood beside him; neither of them spoke a word as the vessel drew closer.

Everything was visible, so close was she now, from the reef points on the great mainsail, luminous with the sunlight, and white as the wing of a gull, to the rail of the bulwarks. A crowd of men were hanging over the port bulwarks gazing at the island and the figures on the reef. Browned by the sun and sea-breeze, Emmeline's hair blowing on the wind, and the point of Dick's javelin flashing in the sun, they looked an ideal pair of savages, seen from the schooner's deck.

"They are going away," said Emmeline, with a long-drawn breath of relief.

Dick made no reply; he stared at the schooner a moment longer in silence, then, having made sure that she was standing away from the land, he began to run up and down, calling out wildly, and beckoning to the vessel as if to call her back.

A moment later a sound came on the breeze, a faint hail; a flag was run up to the peak and dipped as in derision, and the vessel continued on her course.

As a matter of fact, she had been on the point of putting about. Her captain had for a moment been undecided as to whether the forms on the reef were those of castaways or savages. But the javelin in Dick's hand had turned the scale of his opinion in favour of the theory of savages.

VIII

LOVE STEPS IN

Two birds were sitting in the branches of the artu tree: Koko had taken a mate. They had built a nest out of fibres pulled from the wrappings of the cocoa-nut fronds, bits of stick and wire grass—anything, in fact; even fibres from the palmetto thatch of the house below. The pilferings of birds, the building of nests, what charming incidents they are in the great episode of spring!

The hawthorn tree never bloomed here, the climate was that of eternal summer, yet the spirit of May came just as she comes to the English countryside or the German forest. The doings in the artu branches greatly interested Emmeline.

The love-making and the nest-building were conducted quite in the usual manner, according to rules laid down by Nature and carried out by men and birds. All sorts of quaint sounds came filtering down through the leaves from the branch where the sapphire-coloured lovers sat side by side, or the fork where the nest was beginning to form: croonings and cluckings, sounds like the flirting of a fan, the sounds of a squabble, followed by the sounds that told of the squabble made up. Sometimes after one of these squabbles a pale blue downy feather or two would come floating earthwards, touch the palmetto leaves of the house-roof and cling there, or be blown on to the grass.

It was some days after the appearance of the schooner, and Dick was making ready to go into the woods and pick guavas. He had all the morning been engaged in making a basket to carry them in. In civilisation he would, judging from his mechanical talent, perhaps have been an engineer, building bridges and ships, instead of palmetto-leaf baskets and cane houses—who knows if he would have been happier?

The heat of midday had passed, when, with the basket hanging over his shoulder on a piece of cane, he started for the woods, Emmeline following. The place they were going to always filled her with a vague dread; not for a great deal would she have gone there alone. Dick had discovered it in one of his rambles.

They entered the wood and passed a little well, a well without apparent source or outlet and a bottom of fine white sand. How the sand had formed there, it would be impossible to say; but there it was, and around the margin grew ferns redoubling themselves on the surface of the crystal-clear water. They left this to the right and struck into the heart of the wood. The heat of midday still lurked here; the way was clear, for there was a sort of path between the trees, as if, in very ancient days, there had been a road.

Right across this path, half lost in shadow, half sunlit, the lianas hung their ropes. The hotoo tree, with its powdering of delicate blossoms, here stood, showing its lost loveliness to the sun; in the shade the scarlet hibiscus burned like a flame. Artu and breadfruit trees and cocoa-nut bordered the way.

As they proceeded the trees grew denser and the path more obscure. All at once, rounding a sharp turn, the path ended in a valley carpeted with fern. This was the place that always filled Emmeline with an undefined dread. One side of it was all built up in terraces with huge blocks of stone. Blocks of stone so enormous, that the wonder was how the ancient builders had put them in their places.

Trees grew along the terraces, thrusting their roots between the interstices of the blocks. At their base, slightly tilted forward as if with the sinkage of years, stood a great stone figure roughly carved, thirty feet high at least—mysterious-looking, the very spirit of the place. This figure and the terraces, the valley itself, and the very trees that grew there, inspired Emmeline with deep curiosity and vague fear.

People had been here once; sometimes she could fancy she saw dark shadows moving amidst the trees, and the whisper of the foliage seemed to her to hide voices at times, even as its shadow concealed forms. It was indeed an uncanny place to be alone in even under the broad light of day. All across the Pacific for thousands of miles you find relics of the past, like these scattered through the islands.

These temple places are nearly all the same: great terraces of stone, massive idols, desolation overgrown with foliage. They hint at one religion, and a time when the sea space of the Pacific was a continent, which, sinking slowly through the ages, has left only its higher lands and hill-tops visible in the form of islands. Round these places the woods are thicker than elsewhere, hinting at the presence there, once, of sacred groves. The idols are immense, their faces are vague; the storms and the suns and the rains of the ages have cast over them a veil. The sphinx is understandable and a toy compared to these things, some of which have a stature of fifty feet, whose creation is veiled in absolute mystery—the gods of a people forever and forever lost.

The "stone man" was the name Emmeline had given the idol of the valley; and sometimes at nights, when her thoughts would stray that way, she would picture him standing all alone in the moonlight or starlight staring straight before him.

He seemed forever listening; unconsciously one fell to listening too, and then the valley seemed steeped in a supernatural silence. He was not good to be alone with.

Emmeline sat down amidst the fears just at his base. When one was close up to him he lost the suggestion of life, and was simply a great stone which cast a shadow in the sun.

Dick threw himself down also to rest. Then he rose up and went off amidst the guava bushes, plucking the fruit and filling his basket. Since he had seen the schooner, the white men on her decks, her great masts and sails, and general appearance of freedom and speed and unknown adventure, he had been more than ordinarily glum and restless. Perhaps he connected her in his mind with the far-away vision of the *Northumberland*, and the idea of other places and lands, and the yearning for change the idea of them inspired.

He came back with his basket full of the ripe fruit, gave some to the girl and sat down beside her. When she had finished eating them she took the cane that he used for carrying the basket and held it in her hands. She was bending it in the form of a bow when it slipped, flew out and struck her companion a sharp blow on the side of his face.

Almost on the instant he turned and slapped her on the shoulder. She stared at him for a moment in troubled amazement, a sob came in her throat. Then some veil seemed lifted, some wizard's wand stretched out, some mysterious vial broken. As she looked at him like that, he suddenly and fiercely clasped her in his arms. He held her like this for a moment, dazed, stupefied, not knowing what to do with her. Then her lips told him, for they met his in an endless kiss.

HENRY DE VERE STACPOOLE

IX

The Sleep of Paradise

The moon rose up that evening and shot her silver arrows at the house under the artu tree. The house was empty. Then the moon came across the sea and across the reef.

She lit the lagoon to its dark, dim heart. She lit the coral brains and sand spaces, and the fish, casting their shadows on the sand and the coral. The keeper of the lagoon rose to greet her, and the fin of him broke her reflection on the mirror-like surface into a thousand glittering ripples. She saw the white staring ribs of the form on the reef. Then, peeping over the trees, she looked down into the valley, where the great idol of stone had kept its solitary vigil for five thousand years, perhaps, or more.

At his base, in his shadow, looking as if under his protection, lay two human beings, naked, clasped in each other's arms, and fast asleep. One could scarcely pity his vigil, had it been marked sometimes through the years by such an incident as this. The thing had been conducted just as the birds conduct their love affairs. An affair absolutely natural, absolutely blameless, and without sin.

It was a marriage according to Nature, without feast or guests, consummated with accidental cynicism under the shadow of a religion a thousand years dead.

So happy in their ignorance were they, that they only knew that suddenly life had changed, that the skies and the sea were bluer, and that they had become in some magical way one a part of the other. The birds on the tree above were equally as happy in their ignorance, and in their love.

PART II

X

An Island Honeymoon

One day Dick climbed on to the tree above the house, and, driving Madame Koko off the nest upon which she was sitting, peeped in. There were several pale green eggs in it. He did not disturb them, but climbed down again, and the bird resumed her seat as if nothing had happened. Such an occurrence would have terrified a bird used to the ways of men, but here the birds were so fearless and so full of confidence that often they would follow Emmeline in the wood, flying from branch to branch, peering at her through the leaves, lighting quite close to her—once, even, on her shoulder.

The days passed. Dick had lost his restlessness: his wish to wander had vanished. He had no reason to wander; perhaps that was the reason why. In all the broad earth he could not have found anything more desirable than what he had.

Instead now of finding a half-naked savage followed dog-like by his mate, you would have found of an evening a pair of lovers wandering on the reef. They had in a pathetic sort of way attempted to adorn the house with a blue flowering creeper taken from the wood and trained over the entrance.

Emmeline, up to this, had mostly done the cooking, such as it was; Dick helped her now, always. He talked to her no longer in short sentences flung out as if to a dog; and she, almost losing the strange reserve that had clung to her from childhood, half showed him her mind. It was a curious mind: the mind of a dreamer, almost the mind of a poet. The Cluricaunes dwelt there, and vague shapes born of things she had heard about or dreamt of: she had thoughts about the sea and stars, the flowers and birds.

Dick would listen to her as she talked, as a man might listen to the sound of a rivulet. His practical mind could take no share in the dreams of his other half, but her conversation pleased him.

He would look at her for a long time together, absorbed in thought. He was admiring her.

Her hair, blue-black and glossy, tangled him in its meshes; he would stroke it, so to speak, with his eyes, and then pull her close to him and bury his face in it; the smell of it was intoxicating. He breathed her as one does the perfume of a rose.

Her ears were small, and like little white shells. He would take one between finger and thumb and play with it as if it were a toy, pulling at the lobe of it, or trying to flatten out the curved part. Her breasts, her shoulders, her knees, her little feet, every bit of her, he would examine and play with and kiss. She would lie and let him, seeming absorbed in some far-away thought, of which he was the object, then all at once her arms would go round him. All this used to go on in the broad light of day, under the shadow of the artu leaves, with no one to watch except the bright-eyed birds in the leaves above.

Not all their time would be spent in this fashion. Dick was just as keen after the fish. He dug up with a spade—improvised from one of the boards of the dinghy—a space of soft earth near the taro patch and planted the seeds of melons he found in the wood; he rethatched the house. They were, in short, as busy as they could be in such a climate, but love-making would come on them in fits, and then everything would be forgotten. Just as one revisits some spot to renew the memory of a painful or pleasant experience received there, they would return to the valley of the idol and spend a whole afternoon in its shade. The absolute happiness of wandering through the woods together, discovering new flowers, getting lost, and finding their way again, was a thing beyond expression.

Dick had suddenly stumbled upon Love. His courtship had lasted only some twenty minutes; it was being gone over again now, and extended.

One day, hearing a curious noise from the tree above the house, he climbed it. The noise came from the nest, which had been temporarily left by the mother bird. It was a gasping, wheezing sound, and it came from four wide-open beaks, so anxious to be fed that one could almost see into the very crops of the owners. They were Koko's children. In another year each of those ugly downy things would, if permitted to live, be a beautiful sapphire-coloured bird with a few dove-coloured tail feathers, coral beak, and bright, intelligent eyes. A few days ago each of these things was imprisoned in a pale green egg. A month ago they were nowhere.

Something hit Dick on the cheek. It was the mother bird returned with food for the young ones. Dick drew his head aside, and she proceeded without more ado to fill their crops.

XI

The Vanishing of Emmeline

Months passed away. Only one bird remained in the branches of the artu: Koko's children and mate had vanished, but he remained. The breadfruit leaves had turned from green to pale gold and darkest amber, and now the new green leaves were being presented to the spring.

Dick, who had a complete chart of the lagoon in his head, and knew all the soundings and best fishing places, the locality of the stinging coral, and the places where you could wade right across at low tide—Dick, one morning, was gathering his things together for a fishing expedition. The place he was going to lay some two and a half miles away across the island, and as the road was bad he was going alone.

Emmeline had been passing a new thread through the beads of the necklace she sometimes wore. This necklace had a history. In the shallows not far away, Dick had found a bed of shell-fish; wading out at low tide, he had taken some of them out to examine. They were oysters. The first one he opened, so disgusting did its appearance seem to him, might have been the last, only that under the beard of the thing lay a pearl. It was about twice the size of a large pea, and so lustrous that even he could not but admire its beauty, though quite unconscious of its value.

He flung the unopened oysters down, and took the thing to Emmeline. Next day, returning by chance to the same spot, he found the oysters he had cast down all dead and open in the sun. He examined them, and found another pearl embedded in one of them. Then he collected nearly a bushel of the oysters, and left them to die and open. The idea had occurred to him of making a necklace for his companion. She had one made of shells, he intended to make her one of pearls.

It took a long time, but it was something to do. He pierced them with a big needle, and at the end of four months or so the thing was complete. Great pearls most of them were—pure white, black, pink, some perfectly round, some tear shaped, some irregular. The thing was worth fifteen, or perhaps twenty thousand pounds, for he only used the biggest he could find, casting away the small ones as useless.

Emmeline this morning had just finished restringing them on a double thread. She looked pale and not at all well and had been restless all night.

As he went off, armed with his spear and fishing tackle, she waved her hand to him without getting up. Usually she followed him a bit into the wood when he was going away like this, but this morning she just sat at the doorway of the little house, the necklace in her lap, following him with her eyes until he was lost amidst the trees.

He had no compass to guide him, and he needed none. He knew the woods by heart. The mysterious line beyond which scarcely an artu tree was to be found. The long strip of mammee apple—a regular sheet of it a hundred yards broad, and reaching from the middle of the island right down to the lagoon. The clearings, some almost circular where the ferns grew knee-deep. Then he came to the bad part.

The vegetation here had burst into a riot. All sorts of great sappy stalks of unknown plants barred the way and tangled the foot; and there were boggy places into which one sank horribly. Pausing to wipe one's brow, the stalks and tendrils one had beaten down, or beaten aside, rose up and closed together, making one a prisoner almost as closely surrounded as a fly in amber.

All the noontides that had ever fallen upon the island seemed to have left some of their heat behind them here. The air was damp and close like the air of a laundry; and the mournful and perpetual buzz of insects filled the silence without destroying it.

A hundred men with scythes might make a road through the place today; a month or two later, searching for the road, you would find none—the vegetation would have closed in as water closes when divided.

This was the haunt of the jug orchid—a veritable jug, lid and all. Raising the lid you would find the jug half filled with water. Sometimes in the tangle up above, between two trees, you would see a thing like a bird come to ruin. Orchids grew here as in a hothouse. All the trees—the few there were—had a spectral and miserable appearance. They were half starved by the voluptuous growth of the gigantic weeds.

If one had much imagination one felt afraid in this place, for one felt not alone. At any moment it seemed that one might be touched on the elbow by a hand reaching out from the surrounding tangle. Even Dick felt this, unimaginative and fearless as he was. It took him nearly three-quarters of an hour to get through, and then, at last, came the blessed air of real day, and a glimpse of the lagoon between the tree-boles.

　　　　　　　　HENRY DE VERE STACPOOLE

He would have rowed round in the dinghy, only that at low tide the shallows of the north of the island were a bar to the boat's passage. Of course he might have rowed all the way round by way of the strand and reef entrance, but that would have meant a circuit of six miles or more. When he came between the trees down to the lagoon edge it was about eleven o'clock in the morning, and the tide was nearly at the full.

The lagoon just here was like a trough, and the reef was very near, scarcely a quarter of a mile from the shore. The water did not shelve, it went down sheer fifty fathoms or more, and one could fish from the bank just as from a pier head. He had brought some food with him, and he placed it under a tree whilst he prepared his line, which had a lump of coral for a sinker. He baited the hook, and whirling the sinker round in the air sent it flying out a hundred feet from shore. There was a baby cocoa-nut tree growing just at the edge of the water. He fastened the end of his line round the narrow stem, in case of eventualities, and then, holding the line itself, he fished.

He had promised Emmeline to return before sundown.

He was a fisherman. That is to say, a creature with the enduring patience of a cat, tireless and heedless of time as an oyster. He came here for sport more than for fish. Large things were to be found in this part of the lagoon. The last time he had hooked a horror in the form of a cat-fish; at least in outward appearance it was likest to a Mississippi cat-fish. Unlike the cat-fish, it was coarse and useless as food, but it gave good sport.

The tide was now going out, and it was at the going-out of the tide that the best fishing was to be had. There was no wind, and the lagoon lay like a sheet of glass, with just a dimple here and there where the outgoing tide made a swirl in the water.

As he fished he thought of Emmeline and the little house under the trees. Scarcely one could call it thinking. Pictures passed before his mind's eye—pleasant and happy pictures, sunlit, moonlit, starlit.

Three hours passed thus without a bite or symptom that the lagoon contained anything else but sea water, and disappointment; but he did not grumble. He was a fisherman. Then he left the line tied to the tree and sat down to eat the food he had brought with him. He had scarcely finished his meal when the baby cocoa-nut tree shivered and became convulsed, and he did not require to touch the taut line to know that it was useless to attempt to cope with the thing at the end of it. The only course was to let it tug and drown itself. So he sat down and watched.

After a few minutes the line slackened, and the little cocoa-nut tree resumed its attitude of pensive meditation and repose. He pulled the line up: there was nothing at the end of it but a hook. He did not grumble; he baited the hook again, and flung it in, for it was quite likely that the ferocious thing in the water would bite again.

Full of this idea and heedless of time he fished and waited. The sun was sinking into the west—he did not heed it. He had quite forgotten that he had promised Emmeline to return before sunset; it was nearly sunset now. Suddenly, just behind him, from among the trees, he heard her voice, crying:

"Dick!"

XII

The Vanishing of Emmeline (continued)

He dropped the line, and turned with a start. There was no one visible. He ran amongst the trees calling out her name, but only echoes answered. Then he came back to the lagoon edge.

He felt sure that what he had heard was only fancy, but it was nearly sunset, and more than time to be off. He pulled in his line, wrapped it up, took his fish-spear and started.

It was just in the middle of the bad place that dread came to him. What if anything had happened to her? It was dusk here, and never had the weeds seemed so thick, dimness so dismal, the tendrils of the vines so gin-like. Then he lost his way—he who was so sure of his way always! The hunter's instinct had been crossed, and for a time he went hither and thither helpless as a ship without a compass. At last he broke into the real wood, but far to the right of where he ought to have been. He felt like a beast escaped from a trap, and hurried along, led by the sound of the surf.

When he reached the clear sward that led down to the lagoon the sun had just vanished beyond the sea-line. A streak of red cloud floated like the feather of a flamingo in the western sky close to the sea, and twilight had already filled the world. He could see the house dimly, under the shadow of the trees, and he ran towards it, crossing the sward diagonally.

Always before, when he had been away, the first thing to greet his eyes on his return had been the figure of Emmeline. Either at the lagoon edge or the house door he would find her waiting for him.

She was not waiting for him tonight. When he reached the house she was not there, and he paused, after searching the place, a prey to the most horrible perplexity, and unable for the moment to think or act.

Since the shock of the occurrence on the reef she had been subject at times to occasional attacks of headache; and when the pain was more than she could bear, she would go off and hide. Dick would hunt for her amidst the trees, calling out her name and hallooing. A faint "halloo" would answer when she heard him, and then he would find her under a tree or bush, with her unfortunate head between her hands, a picture of misery.

He remembered this now, and started off along the borders of the wood, calling to her, and pausing to listen. No answer came.

He searched amidst the trees as far as the little well, waking the echoes with his voice; then he came back slowly, peering about him in the deep dusk that now was yielding to the starlight. He sat down before the door of the house, and, looking at him, you might have fancied him in the last stages of exhaustion. Profound grief and profound exhaustion act on the frame very much in the same way. He sat with his chin resting on his chest, his hands helpless. He could hear her voice, still as he heard it over at the other side of the island. She had been in danger and called to him, and he had been calmly fishing, unconscious of it all.

This thought maddened him. He sat up, stared around him and beat the ground with the palms of his hands; then he sprang to his feet and made for the dinghy. He rowed to the reef: the action of a madman, for she could not possibly be there.

There was no moon, the starlight both lit and veiled the world, and no sound but the majestic thunder of the waves. As he stood, the night wind blowing on his face, the white foam seething before him, and Canopus burning in the great silence overhead, the fact that he stood in the centre of an awful and profound indifference came to his untutored mind with a pang.

He returned to the shore: the house was still deserted. A little bowl made from the shell of a cocoa-nut stood on the grass near the doorway. He had last seen it in her hands, and he took it up and held it for a moment, pressing it tightly to his breast. Then he threw himself down before the doorway, and lay upon his face, with head resting upon his arms in the attitude of a person who is profoundly asleep.

He must have searched through the woods again that night just as a somnambulist searches, for he found himself towards dawn in the valley before the idol. Then it was daybreak—the world was full of light and colour. He was seated before the house door, worn out and exhausted, when, raising his head, he saw Emmeline's figure coming out from amidst the distant trees on the other side of the sward.

XIII

THE NEWCOMER

H e could not move for a moment, then he sprang to his feet and ran towards her. She looked pale and dazed, and she held something in her arms; something wrapped up in her scarf. As he pressed her to him, the something in the bundle struggled against his breast and emitted a squall—just like the squall of a cat. He drew back, and Emmeline, tenderly moving her scarf a bit aside, exposed a wee face. It was brick-red and wrinkled; there were two bright eyes, and a tuft of dark hair over the forehead. Then the eyes closed, the face screwed itself up, and the thing sneezed twice.

"Where did you *get* it?" he asked, absolutely lost in astonishment as she covered the face again gently with the scarf.

"I found it in the woods," replied Emmeline.

Dumb with amazement, he helped her along to the house, and she sat down, resting her head against the bamboos of the wall.

"I felt so bad," she explained; "and then I went off to sit in the woods, and then I remembered nothing more, and when I woke up it was there."

"It's a baby!" said Dick.

"I know," replied Emmeline.

Mrs. James's baby, seen in the long ago, had risen up before their mind's eyes, a messenger from the past to explain what the new thing was. Then she told him things—things that completely shattered the old "cabbage bed" theory, supplanting it with a truth far more wonderful, far more poetical, too, to he who can appreciate the marvel and the mystery of life.

"It has something funny tied on to it," she went on, as if she were referring to a parcel she had just received.

"Let's look," said Dick.

"No," she replied; "leave it alone."

She sat rocking the thing gently, seeming oblivious to the whole world, and quite absorbed in it, as, indeed, was Dick. A physician would have shuddered, but, perhaps fortunately enough, there was no physician on the island. Only Nature, and she put everything to rights in her own time and way.

When Dick had sat marvelling long enough, he set to and lit the fire. He had eaten nothing since the day before, and he was nearly as exhausted as the girl. He cooked some breadfruit, there was some cold fish left over from the day before; this, with some bananas, he served up on two broad leaves, making Emmeline eat first.

Before they had finished, the creature in the bundle, as though it had smelt the food, began to scream. Emmeline drew the scarf aside. It looked hungry; its mouth would now be pinched up and now wide open, its eyes opened and closed. The girl touched it on the lips with her finger, and it seized upon her fingertip and sucked it. Her eyes filled with tears, she looked appealingly at Dick, who was on his knees; he took a banana, peeled it, broke off a bit and handed it to her. She approached it to the baby's mouth. It tried to suck it, failed, blew bubbles at the sun and squalled.

"Wait a minute," said Dick.

There were some green cocoa-nuts he had gathered the day before close by. He took one, removed the green husk, and opened one of the eyes, making an opening also in the opposite side of the shell. The unfortunate infant sucked ravenously at the nut, filled its stomach with the young cocoa-nut juice, vomited violently, and wailed. Emmeline in despair clasped it to her naked breast, wherefrom, in a moment, it was hanging like a leech. It knew more about babies than they did.

XIV

HANNAH

At noon, in the shallows of the reef, under the burning sun, the water would be quite warm. They would carry the baby down here, and Emmeline would wash it with a bit of flannel. After a few days it scarcely ever screamed, even when she washed it. It would lie on her knees during the process, striking valiantly out with its arms and legs, staring straight up at the sky. Then, when she turned it on its face, it would lay its head down and chuckle and blow bubbles at the coral of the reef, examining, apparently, the pattern of the coral with deep and philosophic attention.

Dick would sit by with his knees up to his chin, watching it all. He felt himself to be part proprietor in the thing—as indeed he was. The mystery of the affair still hung over them both. A week ago they two had been alone, and suddenly from nowhere this new individual had appeared.

It was so complete. It had hair on its head, tiny finger-nails, and hands that would grasp you. It had a whole host of little ways of its own, and everyday added to them.

In a week the extreme ugliness of the newborn child had vanished. Its face, which had seemed carved in the imitation of a monkey's face from half a brick, became the face of a happy and healthy baby. It seemed to see things, and sometimes it would laugh and chuckle as though it had been told a good joke. Its black hair all came off and was supplanted by a sort of down. It had no teeth. It would lie on its back and kick and crow, and double its fists up and try to swallow them alternately, and cross its feet and play with its toes. In fact, it was exactly like any of the thousand-and-one babies that are born into the world at every tick of the clock.

"What will we call it?" said Dick one day, as he sat watching his son and heir crawling about on the grass under the shade of the breadfruit leaves.

"Hannah," said Emmeline promptly.

The recollection of another baby once heard about was in her mind; and it was as good a name as any other, perhaps, in that lonely place, notwithstanding the fact that Hannah was a boy.

Koko took a vast interest in the new arrival. He would hop round it and peer at it with his head on one side; and Hannah would crawl after the bird and try to grab it by the tail. In a few months so valiant and strong did he become that he would pursue his own father, crawling before him on the grass, and you might have seen the mother and father and child playing all together like three children, the bird sometimes hovering overhead like a good spirit, sometimes joining in the fun.

Sometimes Emmeline would sit and brood over the child, a troubled expression on her face and a far-away look in her eyes. The old vague fear of mischance had returned—the dread of that viewless form her imagination half pictured behind the smile on the face of Nature. Her happiness was so great that she dreaded to lose it.

There is nothing more wonderful than the birth of a man, and all that goes to bring it about. Here, on this island, in the very heart of the sea, amidst the sunshine and the wind-blown trees, under the great blue arch of the sky, in perfect purity of thought, they would discuss the question from beginning to end without a blush, the object of their discussion crawling before them on the grass, and attempting to grab feathers from Koko's tail.

It was the loneliness of the place as well as their ignorance of life that made the old, old miracle appear so strange and fresh—as beautiful as the miracle of death had appeared awful. In thoughts vague and beyond expression in words, they linked this new occurrence with that old occurrence on the reef six years before. The vanishing and the coming of a man.

HANNAH, DESPITE HIS UNFORTUNATE NAME, was certainly a most virile and engaging baby. The black hair which had appeared and vanished like some practical joke played by Nature, gave place to a down at first as yellow as sun-bleached wheat, but in a few months' time tinged with auburn.

One day—he had been uneasy and biting at his thumbs for sometime past—Emmeline, looking into his mouth, saw something white and like a grain of rice protruding from his gum. It was a tooth just born. He could eat bananas now, and breadfruit, and they often fed him on fish—a fact which again might have caused a medical man to shudder; yet he throve on it all, and waxed stouter everyday.

Emmeline, with a profound and natural wisdom, let him crawl about stark naked, dressed in ozone and sunlight. Taking him out on the reef, she would let him paddle in the shallow pools, holding him under the armpits whilst he splashed the diamond-bright water into spray with his feet, and laughed and shouted.

They were beginning now to experience a phenomenon, as wonderful as the birth of the child's body—the birth of his intelligence: the peeping out of a little personality with predilections of its own, likes and dislikes.

He knew Dick from Emmeline; and when Emmeline had satisfied his material wants, he would hold out his arms to go to Dick if he were by. He looked upon Koko as a friend, but when a friend of Koko's—a bird with an inquisitive mind and three red feathers in his tail—dropped in one day to inspect the newcomer, he resented the intrusion, and screamed.

He had a passion for flowers, or anything bright. He would laugh and shout when taken on the lagoon in the dinghy, and make as if to jump into the water to get at the bright-coloured corals below.

Ah me! we laugh at young mothers, and all the miraculous things they tell us about their babies. They see what we cannot see: the first unfolding of that mysterious flower, the mind.

One day they were out on the lagoon. Dick had been rowing; he had ceased, and was letting the boat drift for a bit. Emmeline was dancing the child on her knee, when it suddenly held out its arms to the oarsman and said:

"Dick!"

The little word, so often heard and easily repeated, was its first word on earth.

A voice that had never spoken in the world before, had spoken; and to hear his name thus mysteriously uttered by a being he has created, is the sweetest and perhaps the saddest thing a man can ever know.

Dick took the child on his knee, and from that moment his love for it was more than his love for Emmeline or anything else on earth.

XV

The Lagoon of Fire

E ver since the tragedy of six years ago there had been forming in the mind of Emmeline Lestrange a something—shall I call it a deep mistrust. She had never been clever; lessons had saddened and wearied her, without making her much the wiser. Yet her mind was of that order into which profound truths come by short cuts. She was intuitive.

Great knowledge may lurk in the human mind without the owner of the mind being aware. He or she acts in such or such a way, or thinks in such and such a manner from intuition; in other words, as the outcome of the profoundest reasoning.

When we have learned to call storms, storms, and death, death, and birth, birth; when we have mastered the sailor's horn book, and Mr. Piddington's law of cyclones, Ellis's anatomy, and Lewer's midwifery, we have already made ourselves half blind. We have become hypnotised by words and names. We think in words and names, not in ideas; the commonplace has triumphed, the true intellect is half crushed.

Storms had burst over the island before this. And what Emmeline remembered of them might be expressed by an instance.

The morning would be bright and happy, never so bright the sun, or so balmy the breeze, or so peaceful the blue lagoon; then, with a horrid suddenness, as if sick with dissimulation and mad to show itself, something would blacken the sun, and with a yell stretch out a hand and ravage the island, churn the lagoon into foam, beat down the cocoa-nut trees, and slay the birds. And one bird would be left and another taken, one tree destroyed, and another left standing. The fury of the thing was less fearful than the blindness of it, and the indifference of it.

One night, when the child was asleep, just after the last star was lit, Dick appeared at the doorway of the house. He had been down to the water's edge and had now returned. He beckoned Emmeline to follow him, and, putting down the child, she did so.

"Come here and look," said he.

He led the way to the water; and as they approached it, Emmeline became aware that there was something strange about the lagoon. From a distance it looked pale and solid; it might have been a great stretch of grey marble veined with black. Then, as she drew nearer, she saw that the dull grey appearance was a deception of the eye.

The lagoon was alight and burning.

The phosphoric fire was in its very heart and being; every coral branch was a torch, every fish a passing lantern. The incoming tide moving the waters made the whole glittering floor of the lagoon move and shiver, and the tiny waves to lap the bank, leaving behind them glow-worm traces.

"Look!" said Dick.

He knelt down and plunged his forearm into the water. The immersed part burned like a smouldering torch. Emmeline could see it as plainly as though it were lit by sunlight. Then he drew his arm out, and as far as the water had reached, it was covered by a glowing glove.

They had seen the phosphorescence of the lagoon before; indeed, any night you might watch the passing fish like bars of silver, when the moon was away; but this was something quite new, and it was entrancing.

Emmeline knelt down and dabbled her hands, and made herself a pair of phosphoric gloves, and cried out with pleasure, and laughed. It was all the pleasure of playing with fire without the danger of being burnt. Then Dick rubbed his face with the water till it glowed.

"Wait!" he cried; and, running up to the house, he fetched out Hannah.

He came running down with him to the water's edge, gave Emmeline the child, unmoored the boat, and started out from shore.

The sculls, as far as they were immersed, were like bars of glistening silver; under them passed the fish, leaving cometic tails; each coral clump was a lamp, lending its lustre till the great lagoon was luminous as a lit-up ballroom. Even the child on Emmeline's lap crowed and cried out at the strangeness of the sight.

They landed on the reef and wandered over the flat. The sea was white and bright as snow, and the foam looked like a hedge of fire.

As they stood gazing on this extraordinary sight, suddenly, almost as instantaneously as the switching off of an electric light, the phosphorescence of the sea flickered and vanished.

The moon was rising. Her crest was just breaking from the water, and as her face came slowly into view behind a belt of vapour that lay on the horizon, it looked fierce and red, stained with smoke like the face of Eblis.

XVI

The Cyclone

When they awoke next morning the day was dark. A solid roof of cloud, lead-coloured and without a ripple on it, lay over the sky, almost to the horizon. There was not a breath of wind, and the birds flew wildly about as if disturbed by some unseen enemy in the wood.

As Dick lit the fire to prepare the breakfast, Emmeline walked up and down, holding her baby to her breast; she felt restless and uneasy.

As the morning wore on the darkness increased; a breeze rose up, and the leaves of the breadfruit trees pattered together with the sound of rain falling upon glass. A storm was coming, but there was something different in its approach to the approach of the storms they had already known.

As the breeze increased a sound filled the air, coming from far away beyond the horizon. It was like the sound of a great multitude of people, and yet so faint and vague was it that sudden bursts of the breeze through the leaves above would drown it utterly. Then it ceased, and nothing could be heard but the rocking of the branches and the tossing of the leaves under the increasing wind, which was now blowing sharply and fiercely and with a steady rush dead from the west, fretting the lagoon, and sending clouds and masses of foam right over the reef. The sky that had been so leaden and peaceful and like a solid roof was now all in a hurry, flowing eastward like a great turbulent river in spate.

And now, again, one could hear the sound in the distance—the thunder of the captains of the storm and the shouting; but still so faint, so vague, so indeterminate and unearthly that it seemed like the sound in a dream.

Emmeline sat amidst the ferns on the floor cowed and dumb, holding the baby to her breast. It was fast asleep. Dick stood at the doorway. He was disturbed in mind, but he did not show it.

The whole beautiful island world had now taken on the colour of ashes and the colour of lead. Beauty had utterly vanished, all seemed sadness and distress.

The cocoa-palms, under the wind that had lost its steady rush and was now blowing in hurricane blasts, flung themselves about in all the

HENRY DE VERE STACPOOLE

attitudes of distress; and whoever has seen a tropical storm will know what a cocoa-palm can express by its movements under the lash of the wind.

Fortunately the house was so placed that it was protected by the whole depth of the grove between it and the lagoon; and fortunately, too, it was sheltered by the dense foliage of the breadfruit, for suddenly, with a crash of thunder as if the hammer of Thor had been flung from sky to earth, the clouds split and the rain came down in a great slanting wave. It roared on the foliage above, which, bending leaf on leaf, made a slanting roof from which it rushed in a steady sheet-like cascade.

Dick had darted into the house, and was now sitting beside Emmeline, who was shivering and holding the child, which had awakened at the sound of the thunder.

For an hour they sat, the rain ceasing and coming again, the thunder shaking earth and sea, and the wind passing overhead with a piercing, monotonous cry.

Then all at once the wind dropped, the rain ceased, and a pale spectral light, like the light of dawn, fell before the doorway.

"It's over!" cried Dick, making to get up.

"Oh, listen!" said Emmeline, clinging to him, and holding the baby to his breast as if the touch of him would give it protection. She had divined that there was something approaching worse than a storm.

Then, listening in the silence, away from the other side of the island, they heard a sound like the droning of a great top.

It was the centre of the cyclone approaching.

A cyclone is a circular storm: a storm in the form of a ring. This ring of hurricane travels across the ocean with inconceivable speed and fury, yet its centre is a haven of peace.

As they listened the sound increased, sharpened, and became a tang that pierced the ear-drums: a sound that shook with hurry and speed, increasing, bringing with it the bursting and crashing of trees, and breaking at last overhead in a yell that stunned the brain like the blow of a bludgeon. In a second the house was torn away, and they were clinging to the roots of the breadfruit, deaf, blinded, half-lifeless.

The terror and the prolonged shock of it reduced them from thinking beings to the level of frightened animals whose one instinct is preservation.

How long the horror lasted they could not tell, when, like a madman who pauses for a moment in the midst of his struggles and stands stock-still, the wind ceased blowing, and there was peace. The centre of the cyclone was passing over the island.

Looking up, one saw a marvellous sight. The air was full of birds, butterflies, insects—all hanging in the heart of the storm and travelling with it under its protection.

Though the air was still as the air of a summer's day, from north, south, east, and west, from every point of the compass, came the yell of the hurricane.

There was something shocking in this.

In a storm one is so beaten about by the wind that one has no time to think: one is half stupefied. But in the dead centre of a cyclone one is in perfect peace. The trouble is all around, but it is not here. One has time to examine the thing like a tiger in a cage, listen to its voice and shudder at its ferocity.

The girl, holding the baby to her breast, sat up gasping. The baby had come to no harm; it had cried at first when the thunder broke, but now it seemed impassive, almost dazed. Dick stepped from under the tree and looked at the prodigy in the air.

The cyclone had gathered on its way sea-birds and birds from the land; there were gulls, electric white and black man-of-war birds, butterflies, and they all seemed imprisoned under a great drifting dome of glass. As they went, travelling like things without volition and in a dream, with a hum and a roar the south-west quadrant of the cyclone burst on the island, and the whole bitter business began over again.

It lasted for hours, then towards midnight the wind fell; and when the sun rose next morning he came through a cloudless sky, without a trace of apology for the destruction caused by his children the winds. He showed trees uprooted and birds lying dead, three or four canes remaining of what had once been a house, the lagoon the colour of a pale sapphire, and a glass-green, foam-capped sea racing in thunder against the reef.

HENRY DE VERE STACPOOLE

XVII

THE STRICKEN WOODS

At first they thought they were ruined; then Dick, searching, found the old saw under a tree, and the butcher's knife near it, as though the knife and saw had been trying to escape in company and had failed.

Bit by bit they began to recover something of their scattered property. The remains of the flannel had been taken by the cyclone and wrapped round and round a slender cocoa-nut tree, till the trunk looked like a gaily-bandaged leg. The box of fishhooks had been jammed into the centre of a cooked breadfruit, both having been picked up by the fingers of the wind and hurled against the same tree; and the stay-sail of the *Shenandoah* was out on the reef, with a piece of coral carefully placed on it as if to keep it down. As for the lug-sail belonging to the dinghy, it was never seen again.

There is humour sometimes in a cyclone, if you can only appreciate it; no other form of air disturbance produces such quaint effects. Beside the great main whirlpool of wind, there are subsidiary whirlpools, each actuated by its own special imp.

Emmeline had felt Hannah nearly snatched from her arms twice by these little ferocious gimlet winds; and that the whole business of the great storm was set about with the object of snatching Hannah from her, and blowing him out to sea, was a belief which she held, perhaps, in the innermost recesses of her mind.

The dinghy would have been utterly destroyed, had it not heeled over and sunk in shallow water at the first onset of the wind; as it was, Dick was able to bail it out at the next low tide, when it floated as bravely as ever, not having started a single seam.

But the destruction amidst the trees was pitiful. Looking at the woods as a mass, one noticed gaps here and there, but what had really happened could not be seen till one was amongst the trees. Great, beautiful cocoa-nut palms, not dead, but just dying, lay crushed and broken as if trampled upon by some enormous foot. You would come across half a dozen lianas twisted into one great cable. Where cocoa-nut palms were, you could not move a yard without kicking against a fallen nut; you might have picked up full-grown, half-grown, and wee baby nuts, not bigger than small apples, for on the same tree you will find nuts of all sizes and conditions.

One never sees a perfectly straight-stemmed cocoa-palm; they all have an inclination from the perpendicular more or less; perhaps that is why a cyclone has more effect on them than on other trees.

Artus, once so pretty a picture with their diamond-chequered trunks, lay broken and ruined; and right through the belt of mammee apple, right through the bad lands, lay a broad road, as if an army, horse, foot, and artillery, had passed that way from lagoon edge to lagoon edge. This was the path left by the great fore-foot of the storm; but had you searched the woods on either side, you would have found paths where the lesser winds had been at work, where the baby whirlwinds had been at play.

From the bruised woods, like an incense offered to heaven, rose a perfume of blossoms gathered and scattered, of rain-wet leaves, of lianas twisted and broken and oozing their sap; the perfume of newly-wrecked and ruined trees—the essence and soul of the artu, the banyan and cocoa-palm cast upon the wind.

You would have found dead butterflies in the woods, dead birds too; but in the great path of the storm you would have found dead butterflies' wings, feathers, leaves frayed as if by fingers, branches of the aoa, and sticks of the hibiscus broken into little fragments.

Powerful enough to rip a ship open, root up a tree, half ruin a city. Delicate enough to tear a butterfly wing from wing—that is a cyclone.

Emmeline, wandering about in the woods with Dick on the day after the storm, looking at the ruin of great tree and little bird, and recollecting the land birds she had caught a glimpse of yesterday being carried along safely by the storm out to sea to be drowned, felt a great weight lifting from her heart. Mischance had come, and spared them and the baby. The blue had spoken, but had not called them.

She felt that something—the something which we in civilisation call Fate—was for the present gorged; and, without being annihilated, her incessant hypochondriacal dread condensed itself into a point, leaving her horizon sunlit and clear.

The cyclone had indeed treated them almost, one might say, amiably. It had taken the house—but that was a small matter, for it had left them nearly all their small possessions. The tinder box and flint and steel would have been a much more serious loss than a dozen houses, for, without it, they would have had absolutely no means of making a fire.

If anything, the cyclone had been almost too kind to them; had let them pay off too little of that mysterious debt they owed to the gods.

XVIII

A Fallen Idol

The next day Dick began to rebuild the house. He had fetched the stay-sail from the reef and rigged up a temporary tent.

It was a great business cutting the canes and dragging them out in the open. Emmeline helped; whilst Hannah, seated on the grass, played with the bird that had vanished during the storm, but reappeared the evening after.

The child and the bird had grown fast friends; they were friendly enough even at first, but now the bird would sometimes let the tiny hands clasp him right round his body—at least, as far as the hands would go.

It is a rare experience for a man to hold a tame and unstruggling and unfrightened bird in his hands; next to pressing a woman in his arms, it is the pleasantest tactile sensation he will ever experience, perhaps, in life. He will feel a desire to press it to his heart, if he has such a thing.

Hannah would press Koko to his little brown stomach, as if in artless admission of where his heart lay.

He was an extraordinarily bright and intelligent child. He did not promise to be talkative, for, having achieved the word "Dick," he rested content for a long while before advancing further into the labyrinth of language; but though he did not use his tongue, he spoke in a host of other ways. With his eyes, that were as bright as Koko's, and full of all sorts of mischief; with his hands and feet and the movements of his body. He had a way of shaking his hands before him when highly delighted, a way of expressing nearly all the shades of pleasure; and though he rarely expressed anger, when he did so, he expressed it fully.

He was just now passing over the frontier into toyland. In civilisation he would no doubt have been the possessor of an india-rubber dog or a woolly lamb, but there were no toys here at all. Emmeline's old doll had been left behind when they took flight from the other side of the island, and Dick, a year or so ago, on one of his expeditions, had found it lying half buried in the sand of the beach.

He had brought it back now more as a curiosity than anything else, and they had kept it on the shelf in the house. The cyclone had impaled it on a tree-twig near by, as if in derision; and Hannah, when it was presented to him as a plaything, flung it away from him as if in disgust. But he would play with flowers or bright shells, or bits of coral, making vague patterns with them on the sward.

All the toy lambs in the world would not have pleased him better than those things, the toys of the Troglodyte children—the children of the Stone Age. To clap two oyster shells together and make a noise—what, after all, could a baby want better than that?

One afternoon, when the house was beginning to take some sort of form, they ceased work and went off into the woods; Emmeline carrying the baby, and Dick taking turns with him. They were going to the valley of the idol.

Since the coming of Hannah, and even before, the stone figure standing in its awful and mysterious solitude had ceased to be an object of dread to Emmeline, and had become a thing vaguely benevolent. Love had come to her under its shade; and under its shade the spirit of the child had entered into her—from where, who knows? But certainly through heaven.

Perhaps the thing which had been the god of some unknown people had inspired her with the instinct of religion; if so, she was his last worshipper on earth, for when they entered the valley they found him lying upon his face. Great blocks of stone lay around him: there had evidently been a landslip, a catastrophe preparing for ages, and determined, perhaps, by the torrential rain of the cyclone.

In Ponape, Huahine, in Easter Island, you may see great idols that have been felled like this, temples slowly dissolving from sight, and terraces, seemingly as solid as the hills, turning softly and subtly into shapeless mounds of stone.

XIX

THE EXPEDITION

Next morning the light of day filtering through the trees awakened Emmeline in the tent which they had improvised whilst the house was building. Dawn came later here than on the other side of the island which faced east—later, and in a different manner—for there is the difference of worlds between dawn coming over a wooded hill, and dawn coming over the sea.

Over at the other side, sitting on the sand with the break of the reef which faced the east before you, scarcely would the east change colour before the sea-line would be on fire, the sky lit up into an illimitable void of blue, and the sunlight flooding into the lagoon, the ripples of light seeming to chase the ripples of water.

On this side it was different. The sky would be dark and full of stars, and the woods, great spaces of velvety shadow. Then through the leaves of the artu would come a sigh, and the leaves of the breadfruit would patter, and the sound of the reef become faint. The land breeze had awakened, and in a while, as if it had blown them away, looking up, you would find the stars gone, and the sky a veil of palest blue. In this indirect approach of dawn there was something ineffably mysterious. One could see, but the things seen were indecisive and vague, just as they are in the gloaming of an English summer's day.

Scarcely had Emmeline arisen when Dick woke also, and they went out on to the sward, and then down to the water's edge. Dick went in for a swim, and the girl, holding the baby, stood on the bank watching him.

Always after a great storm the weather of the island would become more bracing and exhilarating, and this morning the air seemed filled with the spirit of spring. Emmeline felt it, and as she watched the swimmer disporting in the water, she laughed, and held the child up to watch him. She was fey. The breeze, filled with all sorts of sweet perfumes from the woods, blew her black hair about her shoulders, and the full light of morning coming over the palm fronds of the woods beyond the sward touched her and the child. Nature seemed caressing them.

Dick came ashore, and then ran about to dry himself in the wind. Then he went to the dinghy and examined her; for he had determined to leave the house-building for half a day, and row round to the old place to see how the banana trees had fared during the storm. His anxiety about them was not to be wondered at. The island was his larder, and the bananas were a most valuable article of food. He had all the feelings of a careful housekeeper about them, and he could not rest till he had seen for himself the extent of damage, if damage there was any.

He examined the boat, and then they all went back to breakfast. Living their lives, they had to use forethought. They would put away, for instance, all the shells of the cocoa-nuts they used for fuel; and you never could imagine the blazing splendour there lives in the shell of a cocoa-nut till you see it burning. Yesterday, Dick, with his usual prudence, had placed a heap of sticks, all wet with the rain of the storm, to dry in the sun: as a consequence, they had plenty of fuel to make a fire with this morning.

When they had finished breakfast he got the knife to cut the bananas with—if there were any left to cut—and, taking the javelin, he went down to the boat, followed by Emmeline and the child.

Dick had stepped into the boat, and was on the point of unmooring her, and pushing her off, when Emmeline stopped him.

"Dick!"

"Yes?"

"I will go with you."

"You!" said he in astonishment.

"Yes, I'm—not afraid anymore."

It was a fact; since the coming of the child she had lost that dread of the other side of the island—or almost lost it.

Death is a great darkness, birth is a great light—they had intermixed in her mind; the darkness was still there, but it was no longer terrible to her, for it was infused with the light. The result was a twilight sad, but beautiful, and unpeopled with forms of fear.

Years ago she had seen a mysterious door close and shut a human being out forever from the world. The sight had filled her with dread unimaginable, for she had no words for the thing, no religion or philosophy to explain it away or gloss it over. Just recently she had seen an equally mysterious door open and admit a human being; and deep down in her mind, in the place where the dreams were, the one great fact had explained and justified the other. Life had vanished into the void, but life had come from there. There was life in the void, and it was no longer terrible.

Perhaps all religions were born on a day when some woman, seated upon a rock by the prehistoric sea, looked at her newborn child and recalled to mind her man who had been slain, thus closing the charm and imprisoning the idea of a future state.

Emmeline, with the child in her arms, stepped into the little boat and took her seat in the stern, whilst Dick pushed off. Scarcely had he put out the sculls than a new passenger arrived. It was Koko. He would often accompany them to the reef, though, strangely enough, he would never go there alone of his own accord. He made a circle or two over them, and then lit on the gunwale in the bow, and perched there, humped up, and with his long dove-coloured tail feathers presented to the water.

The oarsman kept close in-shore, and as they rounded the little cape all gay with wild cocoa-nut the bushes brushed the boat, and the child, excited by their colour, held out his hands to them. Emmeline stretched out her hand and broke off a branch; but it was not a branch of the wild cocoa-nut she had plucked, it was a branch of the never-wake-up berries. The berries that will cause a man to sleep, should he eat of them—to sleep and dream, and never wake up again.

"Throw them away!" cried Dick, who remembered.

"I will in a minute," she replied.

She was holding them up before the child, who was laughing and trying to grasp them. Then she forgot them, and dropped them in the bottom of the boat, for something had struck the keel with a thud, and the water was boiling all round.

There was a savage fight going on below. In the breeding season great battles would take place sometimes in the lagoon, for fish have their jealousies just like men—love affairs, friendships. The two great forms could be dimly perceived, one in pursuit of the other, and they terrified Emmeline, who implored Dick to row on.

They slipped by the pleasant shores that Emmeline had never seen before, having been sound asleep when they came past them those years ago.

Just before putting off she had looked back at the beginnings of the little house under the artu tree, and as she looked at the strange glades and groves, the picture of it rose before her, and seemed to call her back.

It was a tiny possession, but it was home; and so little used to change was she that already a sort of home-sickness was upon her; but it passed away almost as soon as it came, and she fell to wondering at the things around her, and pointing them out to the child.

HENRY DE VERE STACPOOLE

When they came to the place where Dick had hooked the albicore, he hung on his oars and told her about it. It was the first time she had heard of it; a fact which shows into what a state of savagery he had been lapsing. He had mentioned about the canoes, for he had to account for the javelin; but as for telling her of the incidents of the chase, he no more thought of doing so than a red Indian would think of detailing to his squaw the incidents of a bear hunt. Contempt for women is the first law of savagery, and perhaps the last law of some old and profound philosophy.

She listened, and when it came to the incident of the shark, she shuddered.

"I wish I had a hook big enough to catch him with," said he, staring into the water as if in search of his enemy.

"Don't think of him, Dick," said Emmeline, holding the child more tightly to her heart. "Row on."

He resumed the sculls, but you could have seen from his face that he was recounting to himself the incident.

When they had rounded the last promontory, and the strand and the break in the reef opened before them, Emmeline caught her breath. The place had changed in some subtle manner; everything was there as before, yet everything seemed different—the lagoon seemed narrower, the reef nearer, the cocoa-palms not nearly so tall. She was contrasting the real things with the recollection of them when seen by a child. The black speck had vanished from the reef; the storm had swept it utterly away.

Dick beached the boat on the shelving sand, and left Emmeline seated in the stern of it, whilst he went in search of the bananas; she would have accompanied him, but the child had fallen asleep.

Hannah asleep was even a pleasanter picture than when awake. He looked like a little brown Cupid without wings, bow or arrow. He had all the grace of a curled-up feather. Sleep was always in pursuit of him, and would catch him up at the most unexpected moments—when he was at play, or indeed at anytime. Emmeline would sometimes find him with a coloured shell or bit of coral that he had been playing with in his hand fast asleep, a happy expression on his face, as if his mind were pursuing its earthly avocations on some fortunate beach in dreamland.

Dick had plucked a huge breadfruit leaf and given it to her as a shelter from the sun, and she sat holding it over her, and gazing straight before her, over the white, sunlit sands.

The flight of the mind in reverie is not in a direct line. To her, dreaming as she sat, came all sorts of coloured pictures, recalled by the scene before her: the green water under the stern of a ship, and the word *Shenandoah* vaguely reflected on it; their landing, and the little tea-set spread out on the white sand—she could still see the pansies painted on the plates, and she counted in memory the lead spoons; the great stars that burned over the reef at nights; the Cluricaunes and fairies; the cask by the well where the convolvulus blossomed, and the wind-blown trees seen from the summit of the hill—all these pictures drifted before her, dissolving and replacing each other as they went.

There was sadness in the contemplation of them, but pleasure too. She felt at peace with the world. All trouble seemed far behind her. It was as if the great storm that had left them unharmed had been an ambassador from the powers above to assure her of their forbearance, protection, and love.

All at once she noticed that between the boat's bow and the sand there lay a broad, blue, sparkling line. The dinghy was afloat.

HENRY DE VERE STACPOOLE

XX

The Keeper of the Lagoon

The woods here had been less affected by the cyclone than those upon the other side of the island, but there had been destruction enough. To reach the place he wanted, Dick had to climb over felled trees and fight his way through a tangle of vines that had once hung overhead.

The banana trees had not suffered at all; as if by some special dispensation of Providence even the great bunches of fruit had been scarcely injured, and he proceeded to climb and cut them. He cut two bunches, and with one across his shoulder came back down through the trees.

He had got half across the sands, his head bent under the load, when a distant call came to him, and, raising his head, he saw the boat adrift in the middle of the lagoon, and the figure of the girl in the bow of it waving to him with her arm. He saw a scull floating on the water half-way between the boat and the shore, which she had no doubt lost in an attempt to paddle the boat back. He remembered that the tide was going out.

He flung his load aside, and ran down the beach; in a moment he was in the water. Emmeline, standing up in the boat, watched him.

When she found herself adrift, she had made an effort to row back, and in her hurry shipping the sculls she had lost one. With a single scull she was quite helpless, as she had not the art of sculling a boat from the stern. At first she was not frightened, because she knew that Dick would soon return to her assistance; but as the distance between boat and shore increased, a cold hand seemed laid upon her heart. Looking at the shore it seemed very far away, and the view towards the reef was terrific, for the opening had increased in apparent size, and the great sea beyond seemed drawing her to it.

She saw Dick coming out of the wood with the load on his shoulder, and she called to him. At first he did not seem to hear, then she saw him look up, cast the bananas away, and come running down the sand to the water's edge. She watched him swimming, she saw him seize the scull, and her heart gave a great leap of joy.

Towing the scull and swimming with one arm, he rapidly approached the boat. He was quite close, only ten feet away, when Emmeline saw behind him, shearing through the clear, rippling water and advancing with speed, a dark triangle that seemed made of canvas stretched upon a sword point.

FORTY YEARS AGO HE HAD floated adrift on the sea in the form and likeness of a small shabby pine-cone, a prey to anything that might find him. He had escaped the jaws of the dog-fish, and the jaws of the dog-fish are a very wide door; he had escaped the albicore and squid: his life had been one long series of miraculous escapes from death. Out of a billion like him born in the same year, he and a few others only had survived.

For thirty years he had kept the lagoon to himself, as a ferocious tiger keeps a jungle. He had known the palm tree on the reef when it was a seedling, and he had known the reef even before the palm tree was there. The things he had devoured, flung one upon another, would have made a mountain; yet he was as clear of enmity as a sword, as cruel, and as soulless. He was the spirit of the lagoon.

EMMELINE SCREAMED, AND POINTED TO the thing behind the swimmer. He turned, saw it, dropped the oar and made for the boat. She had seized the remaining scull and stood with it poised, then she hurled it blade foremost at the form in the water, now fully visible, and close on its prey.

She could not throw a stone straight, yet the scull went like an arrow to the mark, balking the pursuer and saving the pursued. In a moment more his leg was over the gunwale, and he was saved.

But the scull was lost.

XXI

The Hand of the Sea

There was nothing in the boat that could possibly be used as a paddle; the scull was only five or six yards away, but to attempt to swim to it was certain death, yet they were being swept out to sea. He might have made the attempt, only that on the starboard quarter the form of the shark, gently swimming at the same pace as they were drifting, could be made out only half veiled by the water.

The bird perched on the gunwale seemed to divine their trouble, for he rose in the air, made a circle, and resumed his perch with all his feathers ruffled.

Dick stood in despair, helpless, his hands clasping his head. The shore was drawing away before him, the surf loudening behind him, yet he could do nothing. The island was being taken away from them by the great hand of the sea.

Then, suddenly, the little boat entered the race formed by the confluence of the tides, from the right and left arms of the lagoon; the sound of the surf suddenly increased as though a door had been flung open. The breakers were falling and the sea-gulls crying on either side of them, and for a moment the ocean seemed to hesitate as to whether they were to be taken away into her wastes, or dashed on the coral strand. Only for a moment this seeming hesitation lasted; then the power of the tide prevailed over the power of the swell, and the little boat taken by the current drifted gently out to sea.

Dick flung himself down beside Emmeline, who was seated in the bottom of the boat holding the child to her breast. The bird, seeing the land retreat, and wise in its instinct, rose into the air. It circled thrice round the drifting boat, and then, like a beautiful but faithless spirit, passed away to the shore.

XXII

Together

The island had sunk slowly from sight; at sundown it was just a trace, a stain on the south-western horizon. It was before the new moon, and the little boat lay drifting. It drifted from the light of sunset into a world of vague violet twilight, and now it lay drifting under the stars.

The girl, clasping the baby to her breast, leaned against her companion's shoulder; neither of them spoke. All the wonders in their short existence had culminated in this final wonder, this passing away together from the world of Time. This strange voyage they had embarked on—to where?

Now that the first terror was over they felt neither sorrow nor fear. They were together. Come what might, nothing could divide them; even should they sleep and never wake up, they would sleep together. Had one been left and the other taken!

As though the thought had occurred to them simultaneously, they turned one to the other, and their lips met, their souls met, mingling in one dream; whilst above in the windless heaven space answered space with flashes of siderial light, and Canopus shone and burned like the pointed sword of Azrael.

Clasped in Emmeline's hand was the last and most mysterious gift of the mysterious world they had known—the branch of crimson berries.

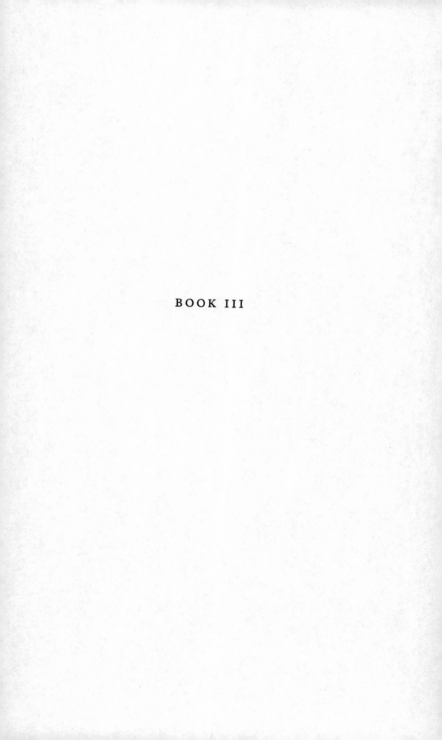

BOOK III

I

MAD LESTRANGE

They knew him upon the Pacific slope as "Mad Lestrange." He was not mad, but he was a man with a fixed idea. He was pursued by a vision: the vision of two children and an old sailor adrift in a little boat upon a wide blue sea.

When the *Arago*, bound for Papetee, picked up the boats of the *Northumberland*, only the people in the long-boat were alive. Le Farge, the captain, was mad, and he never recovered his reason. Lestrange was utterly shattered; the awful experience in the boats and the loss of the children had left him a seemingly helpless wreck. The scowbankers, like all their class, had fared better, and in a few days were about the ship and sitting in the sun. Four days after the rescue the *Arago* spoke the *Newcastle*, bound for San Francisco, and transhipped the shipwrecked men.

Had a physician seen Lestrange on board the *Northumberland* as she lay in that long, long calm before the fire, he would have declared that nothing but a miracle could prolong his life. The miracle came about.

In the general hospital of San Francisco, as the clouds cleared from his mind, they unveiled the picture of the children and the little boat. The picture had been there daily, seen but not truly comprehended; the horrors gone through in the open boat, the sheer physical exhaustion, had merged all the accidents of the great disaster into one mournful half-comprehended fact. When his brain cleared all the other incidents fell out of focus, and memory, with her eyes set upon the children, began to paint a picture that he was ever more to see.

Memory cannot produce a picture that Imagination has not retouched; and her pictures, even the ones least touched by Imagination, are no mere photographs, but the work of an artist. All that is inessential she casts away, all that is essential she retains; she idealises, and that is why her picture of a lost mistress has had power to keep a man a celibate to the end of his days, and why she can break a human heart with the picture of a dead child. She is a painter, but she is also a poet.

The picture before the mind of Lestrange was filled with this almost diabolical poetry, for in it the little boat and her helpless crew were represented adrift on a blue and sunlit sea. A sea most beautiful to look at, yet most terrible, bearing as it did the recollections of thirst.

He had been dying, when, raising himself on his elbow, so to say, he looked at this picture. It recalled him to life. His willpower asserted itself, and he refused to die.

The will of a man has, if it is strong enough, the power to reject death. He was not in the least conscious of the exercise of this power; he only knew that a great and absorbing interest had suddenly arisen in him, and that a great aim stood before him—the recovery of the children.

The disease that was killing him ceased its ravages, or rather was slain in its turn by the increased vitality against which it had to strive. He left the hospital and took up his quarters at the Palace Hotel, and then, like the General of an army, he began to formulate his plan of campaign against Fate.

When the crew of the *Northumberland* had stampeded, hurling their officers aside, lowering the boats with a rush, and casting themselves into the sea, everything had been lost in the way of ship's papers; the charts, the two logs—everything, in fact, that could indicate the latitude and longitude of the disaster. The first and second officers and a midshipman had shared the fate of the quarter-boat; of the foremast hands saved, not one, of course, could give the slightest hint as to the locality of the spot.

A time reckoning from the Horn told little, for there was no record of the log. All that could be said was that the disaster had occurred somewhere south of the line.

In Le Farge's brain lay for a certainty the position, and Lestrange went to see the captain in the "Maison de Sante," where he was being looked after, and found him quite recovered from the furious mania that he had been suffering from. Quite recovered, and playing with a ball of coloured worsted.

There remained the log of the *Arago*; in it would be found the latitude and longitude of the boats she had picked up.

The *Arago*, due at Papetee, became overdue. Lestrange watched the overdue lists from day today, from week to week, from month to month, uselessly, for the *Arago* never was heard of again. One could not affirm even that she was wrecked; she was simply one of the ships that never come back from the sea.

HENRY DE VERE STACPOOLE

II

The Secret of the Azure

To lose a child he loves is undoubtedly the greatest catastrophe that can happen to a man. I do not refer to its death.

A child wanders into the street, or is left by its nurse for a moment, and vanishes. At first the thing is not realised. There is a pang and hurry at the heart which half vanishes, whilst the understanding explains that in a civilised city, if a child gets lost, it will be found and brought back by the neighbours or the police.

But the police know nothing of the matter, or the neighbours, and the hours pass. Any minute may bring back the wanderer; but the minutes pass, and the day wears into evening, and the evening tonight, and the night to dawn, and the common sounds of a new day begin.

You cannot remain at home for restlessness; you go out, only to return hurriedly for news. You are eternally listening, and what you hear shocks you; the common sounds of life, the roll of the carts and cabs in the street, the footsteps of the passers-by, are full of an indescribable mournfulness; music increases your misery into madness, and the joy of others is monstrous as laughter heard in hell.

If someone were to bring you the dead body of the child, you might weep, but you would bless him, for it is the uncertainty that kills.

You go mad, or go on living. Years pass by, and you are an old man. You say to yourself: "He would have been twenty years of age today."

There is not in the old ferocious penal code of our forefathers a punishment adequate to the case of the man or woman who steals a child.

Lestrange was a wealthy man, and one hope remained to him, that the children might have been rescued by some passing ship. It was not the case of children lost in a city, but in the broad Pacific, where ships travel from all ports to all ports, and to advertise his loss adequately it was necessary to placard the world. Ten thousand dollars was the reward offered for news of the lost ones, twenty thousand for the recovery; and the advertisement appeared in every newspaper likely to reach the eyes of a sailor, from the *Liverpool Post* to the *Dead Bird*.

The years passed without anything definite coming in answer to all these advertisements. Once news came of two children saved from the sea in the neighbourhood of the Gilberts, and it was not false news, but they were not the children he was seeking for. This incident at once depressed and stimulated him, for it seemed to say, "If these children have been saved, why not yours?"

The strange thing was, that in his heart he felt a certainty that they were alive. His intellect suggested their death in twenty different forms; but a whisper, somewhere out of that great blue ocean, told him at intervals that what he sought was there, living, and waiting for him.

He was somewhat of the same temperament as Emmeline—a dreamer, with a mind tuned to receive and record the fine rays that fill this world flowing from intellect to intellect, and even from what we call inanimate things. A coarser nature would, though feeling, perhaps, as acutely the grief, have given up in despair the search. But he kept on; and at the end of the fifth year, so far from desisting, he chartered a schooner and passed eighteen months in a fruitless search, calling at little-known islands, and once, unknowing, at an island only three hundred miles away from the tiny island of this story.

If you wish to feel the hopelessness of this unguided search, do not look at a map of the Pacific, but go there. Hundreds and hundreds of thousands of square leagues of sea, thousands of islands, reefs, atolls.

Up to a few years ago there were many small islands utterly unknown; even still there are some, though the charts of the Pacific are the greatest triumphs of hydrography; and though the island of the story was actually on the Admiralty charts, of what use was that fact to Lestrange?

He would have continued searching, but he dared not, for the desolation of the sea had touched him.

In that eighteen months the Pacific explained itself to him in part, explained its vastness, its secrecy and inviolability. The schooner lifted veil upon veil of distance, and veil upon veil lay beyond. He could only move in a right line; to search the wilderness of water with any hope, one would have to be endowed with the gift of moving in all directions at once.

He would often lean over the bulwark rail and watch the swell slip by, as if questioning the water. Then the sunsets began to weigh upon his heart, and the stars to speak to him in a new language, and he knew that it was time to return, if he would return with a whole mind.

When he got back to San Francisco he called upon his agent, Wannamaker of Kearney Street, but there was still no news.

HENRY DE VERE STACPOOLE

III

Captain Fountain

He had a suite of rooms at the Palace Hotel, and he lived the life of any other rich man who is not addicted to pleasure. He knew some of the best people in the city, and conducted himself so sanely in all respects that a casual stranger would never have guessed his reputation for madness; but when you knew him better, you would find sometimes in the middle of a conversation that his mind was away from the subject; and were you to follow him in the street, you would hear him in conversation with himself. Once at a dinner-party he rose and left the room, and did not return. Trifles, but sufficient to establish a reputation of a sort.

One morning—to be precise, it was the second day of May, exactly eight years and five months after the wreck of the *Northumberland*—Lestrange was in his sitting-room reading, when the bell of the telephone, which stood in the corner of the room, rang. He went to the instrument.

"Are you there?" came a high American voice. "Lestrange—right—come down and see me—Wannamaker—I have news for you."

Lestrange held the receiver for a moment, then he put it back in the rest. He went to a chair and sat down, holding his head between his hands, then he rose and went to the telephone again; but he dared not use it, he dare not shatter the newborn hope.

"News!" What a world lies in that word.

In Kearney Street he stood before the door of Wannamaker's office collecting himself and watching the crowd drifting by, then he entered and went up the stairs. He pushed open a swing-door and entered a great room. The clink and rattle of a dozen typewriters filled the place, and all the hurry of business; clerks passed and came with sheaves of correspondence in their hands; and Wannamaker himself, rising from bending over a message which he was correcting on one of the typewriters' tables, saw the newcomer and led him to the private office.

"What is it?" said Lestrange.

"Only this," said the other, taking up a slip of paper with a name and address on it. "Simon J. Fountain, of 45 Rathray Street, West—that's down near the wharves—says he has seen your ad. in an old number of a paper, and he thinks he can tell you something. He did not specify the nature of the intelligence, but it might be worth finding out."

"I will go there," said Lestrange.

"Do you know Rathray Street?"

"No."

Wannamaker went out and called a boy and gave him some directions; then Lestrange and the boy started.

Lestrange left the office without saying "Thank you," or taking leave in anyway of the advertising agent—who did not feel in the least affronted, for he knew his customer.

Rathray Street is, or was before the earthquake, a street of small clean houses. It had a seafaring look that was accentuated by the marine perfumes from the wharves close by and the sound of steam winches loading or discharging cargo—a sound that ceased not night or day as the work went on beneath the sun or the sizzling arc lamps.

No. 45 was almost exactly like its fellows, neither better nor worse; and the door was opened by a neat, prim woman, small, and of middle age. Commonplace she was, no doubt, but not commonplace to Lestrange.

"Is Mr. Fountain in?" he asked. "I have come about the advertisement."

"Oh, have you, sir?" she replied, making way for him to enter, and showing him into a little sitting-room on the left of the passage. "The Captain is in bed; he is a great invalid, but he was expecting, perhaps, someone would call, and he will be able to see you in a minute, if you don't mind waiting."

"Thanks," said Lestrange; "I can wait."

He had waited eight years, what mattered a few minutes now? But at no time in the eight years had he suffered such suspense, for his heart knew that now, just now in this commonplace little house, from the lips of, perhaps, the husband of that commonplace woman, he was going to learn either what he feared to hear, or what he hoped.

It was a depressing little room; it was so clean, and looked as though it were never used. A ship imprisoned in a glass bottle stood upon the mantelpiece, and there were shells from far-away places, pictures of ships in sand—all the things one finds as a rule adorning an old sailor's home.

Lestrange, as he sat waiting, could hear movements from the next room—probably the invalid's, which they were preparing for his reception. The distant sounds of the derricks and winches came muffled through the tightly-shut window that looked as though it never had been opened. A square of sunlight lit the upper part of the cheap lace curtain on the right of the window, and repeated its pattern vaguely on the lower part of the wall opposite. Then a bluebottle fly awoke suddenly into life and began to buzz and drum against the window pane, and Lestrange wished that they would come.

A man of his temperament must necessarily, even under the happiest circumstances, suffer in going through the world; the fine fibre always suffers when brought into contact with the coarse. These people were as kindly disposed as anyone else. The advertisement and the face and manners of the visitor might have told them that it was not the time for delay, yet they kept him waiting whilst they arranged bed-quilts and put medicine bottles straight—as if he could see!

At last the door opened, and the woman said:

"Will you step this way, sir?"

She showed him into a bedroom opening off the passage. The room was neat and clean, and had that indescribable appearance which marks the bedroom of the invalid.

In the bed, making a mountain under the counterpane with an enormously distended stomach, lay a man, black-bearded, and with his large, capable, useless hands spread out on the coverlet—hands ready and willing, but debarred from work. Without moving his body, he turned his head slowly and looked at the newcomer. This slow movement was not from weakness or disease, it was the slow, emotionless nature of the man speaking.

"This is the gentleman, Silas," said the woman, speaking over Lestrange's shoulder. Then she withdrew and closed the door.

"Take a chair, sir," said the sea captain, flapping one of his hands on the counterpane as if in wearied protest against his own helplessness. "I haven't the pleasure of your name, but the missus tells me you're come about the advertisement I lit on yester-even."

He took a paper, folded small, that lay beside him, and held it out to his visitor. It was a *Sidney Bulletin* three years old.

"Yes," said Lestrange, looking at the paper; "that is my advertisement."

"Well, it's strange—very strange," said Captain Fountain, "that I should have lit on it only yesterday. I've had it all three years in my chest, the way old papers get lying at the bottom with odds and ends. Mightn't a' seen it now, only the missus cleared the raffle out of the chest, and, 'Give me that paper,' I says, seeing it in her hand; and I fell to reading it, for a man'll read anything bar tracts lying in bed eight months, as I've been with the dropsy. I've been whaler man and boy forty year, and my last ship was the *Sea-Horse*. Over seven years ago one of my men picked up something on a beach of one of them islands east of the Marquesas—we'd put in to water—"

"Yes, yes," said Lestrange. "What was it he found?"

"Missus!" roared the captain in a voice that shook the walls of the room.

The door opened, and the woman appeared.

"Fetch me my keys out of my trousers pocket."

The trousers were hanging up on the back of the door, as if only waiting to be put on. The woman fetched the keys, and he fumbled over them and found one. He handed it to her, and pointed to the drawer of a bureau opposite the bed.

She knew evidently what was wanted, for she opened the drawer and produced a box, which she handed to him. It was a small cardboard box tied round with a bit of string. He undid the string, and disclosed a child's tea service: a teapot, cream jug, six little plates—all painted with a pansy.

It was the box which Emmeline had always been losing—lost again.

Lestrange buried his face in his hands. He knew the things. Emmeline had shown them to him in a burst of confidence. Out of all that vast ocean he had searched unavailingly: they had come to him like a message, and the awe and mystery of it bowed him down and crushed him.

The captain had placed the things on the newspaper spread out by his side, and he was unrolling the little spoons from their tissue-paper covering. He counted them as if entering up the tale of some trust, and placed them on the newspaper.

"When did you find them?" asked Lestrange, speaking with his face still covered.

"A matter of over seven years ago," replied the captain, "we'd put in to water at a place south of the line—Palm Tree Island we whalemen call it, because of the tree at the break of the lagoon. One of my men brought it aboard, found it in a shanty built of sugar-canes which the men bust up for devilment."

"Good God!" said Lestrange. "Was there no one there—nothing but this box?"

"Not a sight or sound, so the men said; just the shanty abandoned seemingly. I had no time to land and hunt for castaways, I was after whales."

"How big is the island?"

"Oh, a fairish middle-sized island—no natives. I've heard tell it's *tabu*; why, the Lord only knows—some crank of the Kanakas, I s'pose. Anyhow, there's the findings—you recognise them?"

"I do."

"Seems strange," said the captain, "that I should pick 'em up; seems strange your advertisement out, and the answer to it lying amongst my gear, but that's the way things go."

"Strange!" said the other. "It's more than strange."

"Of course," continued the captain, "they might have been on the island hid away som'ere, there's no saying; only appearances are against it. Of course they might be there now unbeknownst to you or me."

"They *are* there now," answered Lestrange, who was sitting up and looking at the playthings as though he read in them some hidden message. "They *are* there now. Have you the position of the island?"

"I have. Missus, hand me my private log."

She took a bulky, greasy, black note-book from the bureau, and handed it to him. He opened it, thumbed the pages, and then read out the latitude and longitude.

"I entered it on the day of finding—here's the entry. 'Adams brought aboard child's toy box out of deserted shanty, which men pulled down; traded it to me for a caulker of rum.' The cruise lasted three years and eight months after that; we'd only been out three when it happened. I forgot all about it: three years scrubbing round the world after whales doesn't brighten a man's memory. Right round we went, and paid off at Nantucket. Then, after a fortni't on shore and a month repairin', the old *Sea-Horse* was off again, I with her. It was at Honolulu this dropsy took me, and back I come here, home. That's the yarn. There's not much to it, but, seein' your advertisement, I thought I might answer it."

Lestrange took Fountain's hand and shook it.

"You see the reward I offered?" he said. "I have not my cheque book with me, but you shall have the cheque in an hour from now."

"No, *sir*," replied the captain; "if anything comes of it, I don't say I'm not open to some small acknowledgment, but ten thousand dollars for a five-cent box—that's not my way of doing business."

"I can't make you take the money now—I can't even thank you properly now," said Lestrange—"I am in a fever; but when all is settled, you and I will settle this business. My God!"

He buried his face in his hands again.

"I'm not wishing to be inquisitive," said Captain Fountain, slowly putting the things back in the box and tucking the paper shavings round them, "but may I ask how you propose to move in this business?"

"I will hire a ship at once and search."

"Ay," said the captain, wrapping up the little spoons in a meditative manner; "perhaps that will be best."

He felt certain in his own mind that the search would be fruitless, but he did not say so. If he had been absolutely certain in his mind without being able to produce the proof, he would not have counselled Lestrange to any other course, knowing that the man's mind would never be settled until proof positive was produced.

"The question is," said Lestrange, "what is my quickest way to get there?"

"There I may be able to help you," said Fountain, tying the string round the box. "A schooner with good heels to her is what you want; and, if I'm not mistaken, there's one discharging cargo at this present minit at O'Sullivan's wharf. Missus!"

The woman answered the call. Lestrange felt like a person in a dream, and these people who were interesting themselves in his affairs seemed to him beneficent beyond the nature of human beings.

"Is Captain Stannistreet home, think you?"

"I don't know," replied the woman; "but I can go see."

"Do."

She went.

"He lives only a few doors down," said Fountain, "and he's the man for you. Best schooner captain ever sailed out of 'Frisco. The *Raratonga* is the name of the boat I have in my mind—best boat that ever wore copper. Stannistreet is captain of her, owners are M'Vitie. She's been missionary, and she's been pigs; copra was her last cargo, and she's nearly discharged it. Oh, M'Vitie would hire her out to Satan at a price; you needn't be afraid of their boggling at it if you can raise the dollars. She's had a new suit of sails only the beginning of the year. Oh, she'll fix you up to a T, and you take the word of S. Fountain for that. I'll engineer the thing from this bed if you'll let me put my oar in your trouble; I'll victual her, and find a crew three quarter price of any of those d—d skulking agents. Oh, I'll take a commission right enough, but I'm half paid with doing the thing—"

He ceased, for footsteps sounded in the passage outside, and Captain Stannistreet was shown in. He was a young man of not more than thirty,

HENRY DE VERE STACPOOLE

alert, quick of eye, and pleasant of face. Fountain introduced him to Lestrange, who had taken a fancy to him at first sight.

When he heard about the business in hand, he seemed interested at once; the affair seemed to appeal to him more than if it had been a purely commercial matter, such as copra and pigs.

"If you'll come with me, sir, down to the wharf, I'll show you the boat now," he said, when they had discussed the matter and threshed it out thoroughly.

He rose, bid good-day to his friend Fountain, and Lestrange followed him, carrying the brown-paper box in his hand.

O'Sullivan's Wharf was not far away. A tall Cape Horner that looked almost a twin sister of the ill-fated *Northumberland* was discharging iron, and astern of her, graceful as a dream, with snow-white decks, lay the *Raratonga* discharging copra.

"That's the boat," said Stannistreet; "cargo nearly all out. How does she strike your fancy?"

"I'll take her," said Lestrange, "cost what it will."

IV

DUE SOUTH

It was on the 10th of May, so quickly did things move under the supervision of the bedridden captain, that the *Raratonga*, with Lestrange on board, cleared the Golden Gates, and made south, heeling to a ten-knot breeze.

There is no mode of travel to be compared to your sailing-ship. In a great ship, if you have ever made a voyage in one, the vast spaces of canvas, the sky-high spars, the *finesse* with which the wind is met and taken advantage of, will form a memory never to be blotted out.

A schooner is the queen of all rigs; she has a bounding buoyancy denied to the square-rigged craft, to which she stands in the same relationship as a young girl to a dowager; and the *Raratonga* was not only a schooner, but the queen, acknowledged of all the schooners in the Pacific.

For the first few days they made good way south; then the wind became baffling and headed them off.

Added to Lestrange's feverish excitement there was an anxiety, a deep and soul-fretting anxiety, as if some half-heard voice were telling him that the children he sought were threatened by some danger.

These baffling winds blew upon the smouldering anxiety in his breast, as wind blows upon embers, causing them to glow. They lasted some days, and then, as if Fate had relented, up sprang on the starboard quarter a spanking breeze, making the rigging sing to a merry tune, and blowing the spindrift from the forefoot, as the *Raratonga*, heeling to its pressure, went humming through the sea, leaving a wake spreading behind her like a fan.

It took them along five hundred miles, silently and with the speed of a dream. Then it ceased.

The ocean and the air stood still. The sky above stood solid like a great pale blue dome; just where it met the water line of the far horizon a delicate tracery of cloud draped the entire round of the sky.

I have said that the ocean stood still as well as the air: to the eye it was so, for the swell under-running the glitter on its surface was so even, so equable, and so rhythmical, that the surface seemed not in motion. Occasionally a dimple broke the surface, and strips of dark sea-weed floated by, showing up the green; dim things rose to the surface, and, guessing the presence of man, sank slowly and dissolved from sight.

Two days, never to be recovered, passed, and still the calm continued. On the morning of the third day it breezed up from the nor'-nor'west, and they continued their course, a cloud of canvas, every sail drawing, and the music of the ripple under the forefoot.

Captain Stannistreet was a genius in his profession; he could get more speed out of a schooner than any other man afloat, and carry more canvas without losing a stick. He was also, fortunately for Lestrange, a man of refinement and education, and what was better still, understanding.

They were pacing the deck one afternoon, when Lestrange, who was walking with his hands behind him, and his eyes counting the brown dowels in the cream-white planking, broke silence.

"You don't believe in visions and dreams?"

"How do you know that?" replied the other.

"Oh, I only put it as a question; most people say they don't."

"Yes, but most people do."

"I do," said Lestrange.

He was silent for a moment.

"You know my trouble so well that I won't bother you going over it, but there has come over me of late a feeling—it is like a waking dream."

"Yes?"

"I can't quite explain, for it is as if I saw something which my intelligence could not comprehend, or make an image of."

"I think I know what you mean."

"I don't think you do. This is something quite strange. I am fifty, and in fifty years a man has experienced, as a rule, all the ordinary and most of the extraordinary sensations that a human being can be subjected to. Well, I have never felt this sensation before; it comes on only at times. I see, as you might imagine, a young baby sees, and things are before me that I do not comprehend. It is not through my bodily eyes that this sensation comes, but through some window of the mind, from before which a curtain has been drawn."

"That's strange," said Stannistreet, who did not like the conversation over-much, being simply a schooner captain and a plain man, though intelligent enough and sympathetic.

"This something tells me," went on Lestrange, "that there is danger threatening the—" He ceased, paused a minute, and then, to Stannistreet's relief, went on. "If I talk like that you will think I am not right in my head: let us pass the subject by, let us forget dreams and omens and come to realities. You know how I lost the children; you know how I hope to find them at the place where Captain Fountain found their traces? He says the island was uninhabited, but he was not sure."

"No," replied Stannistreet, "he only spoke of the beach."

"Yes. Well, suppose there were natives at the other side of the island who had taken these children."

"If so, they would grow up with the natives."

"And become savages?"

"Yes; but the Polynesians can't be really called savages; they are a very decent lot. I've knocked about amongst them a good while, and a kanaka is as white as a white man—which is not saying much, but it's something. Most of the islands are civilised now. Of course there are a few that aren't, but still, suppose even that 'savages,' as you call them, had come and taken the children off—"

Lestrange's breath caught, for this was the very fear that was in his heart, though he had never spoken it.

"Well?"

"Well, they would be well treated."

"And brought up as savages?"

"I suppose so."

Lestrange sighed.

"Look here," said the captain; "it's all very well talking, but upon my word I think that we civilised folk put on a lot of airs, and waste a lot of pity on savages."

"How so?"

"What does a man want to be but happy?"

"Yes."

"Well, who is happier than a naked savage in a warm climate? Oh, he's happy enough, and he's not always holding a corroboree. He's a good deal of a gentleman; he has perfect health; he lives the life a man was born to live face to face with Nature. He doesn't see the sun through an office window or the moon through the smoke of factory chimneys; happy and civilised too—but, bless you, where is he? The whites have driven him out; in one or two small islands you may find him still—a crumb or so of him."

"Suppose," said Lestrange, "suppose those children had been brought up face to face with Nature—"

"Yes?"

"Living that free life—"

"Yes?"

"Waking up under the stars"—Lestrange was speaking with his eyes fixed, as if upon something very far away—"going to sleep as the sun sets, feeling the air fresh, like this which blows upon us, all around them. Suppose they were like that, would it not be a cruelty to bring them to what we call civilisation?"

"I think it would," said Stannistreet.

Lestrange said nothing, but continued pacing the deck, his head bowed and his hands behind his back.

One evening at sunset, Stannistreet said:

"We're two hundred and forty miles from the island, reckoning from today's reckoning at noon. We're going all ten knots even with this breeze; we ought to fetch the place this time tomorrow. Before that if it freshens."

"I am greatly disturbed," said Lestrange.

He went below, and the schooner captain shook his head, and, locking his arm round a ratlin, gave his body to the gentle roll of the craft as she stole along, skirting the sunset, splendid, and to the nautical eye full of fine weather.

The breeze was not quite so fresh next morning, but it had been blowing fairly all the night, and the *Raratonga* had made good way. About eleven it began to fail. It became the lightest sailing breeze, just sufficient to keep the sails drawing, and the wake rippling and swirling behind. Suddenly Stannistreet, who had been standing talking to Lestrange, climbed a few feet up the mizzen ratlins, and shaded his eyes.

"What is it?" asked Lestrange.

"A boat," he replied. "Hand me that glass you will find in the sling there."

He levelled the glass, and looked for a long time without speaking.

"It's a boat adrift—a small boat, nothing in her. Stay! I see something white, can't make it out. Hi there!"—to the fellow at the wheel "Keep her a point more to starboard." He got on to the deck. "We're going dead on for her."

"Is there anyone in her?" asked Lestrange.

"Can't quite make out, but I'll lower the whale-boat and fetch her alongside."

He gave orders for the whale-boat to be slung out and manned.

As they approached nearer, it was evident that the drifting boat, which looked like a ship's dinghy, contained something, but what, could not be made out.

When he had approached near enough, Stannistreet put the helm down and brought the schooner to, with her sails all shivering. He took his place in the bow of the whale-boat and Lestrange in the stern. The boat was lowered, the falls cast off, and the oars bent to the water.

The little dinghy made a mournful picture as she floated, looking scarcely bigger than a walnut shell. In thirty strokes the whale-boat's nose was touching her quarter. Stannistreet grasped her gunwale.

In the bottom of the dinghy lay a girl, naked all but for a strip of coloured striped material. One of her arms was clasped round the neck of a form that was half hidden by her body, the other clasped partly to herself, partly to her companion, the body of a baby. They were natives, evidently, wrecked or lost by some mischance from some inter-island schooner. Their breasts rose and fell gently, and clasped in the girl's hand was a branch of some tree, and on the branch a single withered berry.

"Are they dead?" asked Lestrange, who divined that there were people in the boat, and who was standing up in the stern of the whale-boat trying to see.

"No," said Stannistreet; "they are asleep."

THE END

A Note About the Author

Henry De Vere Stacpoole (1863–1951) was an Irish novelist. Born in Kingstown, Ireland—now Dún Laoghaire—Stacpoole served as a ship's doctor in the South Pacific Ocean as a young man. His experiences on the other side of the world would inspire much of his literary work, including his revered romance novel *The Blue Lagoon* (1908). Stacpoole wrote dozens of novels throughout his career, many of which have served as source material for feature length films. He lived in rural Essex before settling on the Isle of Wight in the 1920s, where he spent the remainder of his life.

A Note from the Publisher

Spanning many genres, from non-fiction essays to literature classics to children's books and lyric poetry, Mint Edition books showcase the master works of our time in a modern new package. The text is freshly typeset, is clean and easy to read, and features a new note about the author in each volume. Many books also include exclusive new introductory material. Every book boasts a striking new cover, which makes it as appropriate for collecting as it is for gift giving. Mint Edition books are only printed when a reader orders them, so natural resources are not wasted. We're proud that our books are never manufactured in excess and exist only in the exact quantity they need to be read and enjoyed.

Discover more of your favorite classics with Bookfinity™.

- Track your reading with custom book lists.
- Get great book recommendations for your personalized Reader Type.
- Add reviews for your favorite books.
- AND MUCH MORE!

Visit **bookfinity.com** and take the fun Reader Type quiz to get started.

Enjoy our classic and modern companion pairings!